Church Choir Mysteries™

The Wicked Step-Twister

Sandy Dengler

Thorndike Press • Waterville, Maine

Copyright © 2000 by Guideposts, Carmel, New York 10512.

Published in 2005 by arrangement with
Guideposts Book Division.

Thorndike Press® Large Print Christian Mystery.

The tree indicium is a trademark of Thorndike Press.

The text of this Large Print edition is unabridged.
Other aspects of the book may vary from the original edition.

Set in 16 pt. Plantin by Carleen Stearns.

Printed in the United States on permanent paper.

Library of Congress Cataloging-in-Publication Data

Dengler, Sandy.
    The wicked step-twister : church choir mysteries / by
Sandy Dengler.
        p. cm. — (Thorndike Press large print Christian
mystery)
    ISBN 0-7862-7780-7 (lg. print : hc : alk. paper)
    1. Church musicians — Fiction. 2. Choirs (Music) —
Fiction. 3. Large type books. I. Title. II. Thorndike
Press large print Christian mystery series.
PS3554.E524W53 2005
    13′.54—dc22
                                                    2005010230

The Wicked Step-Twister

*Also by Sandy Dengler
in Large Print:*

A Model Murder
The Comatose Cat
Murder on the Mount

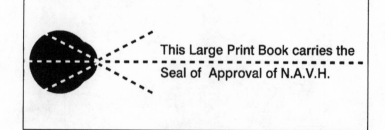

This Large Print Book carries the
Seal of Approval of N.A.V.H.

For Bill,
the sails and rudder on my ship.

As the Founder/CEO of NAVH, the only national health agency solely devoted to those who, although not totally blind, have an eye disease which could lead to serious visual impairment, I am pleased to recognize Thorndike Press* as one of the leading publishers in the large print field.

Founded in 1954 in San Francisco to prepare large print textbooks for partially seeing children, NAVH became the pioneer and standard setting agency in the preparation of large type.

Today, those publishers who meet our standards carry the prestigious "Seal of Approval" indicating high quality large print. We are delighted that Thorndike Press is one of the publishers whose titles meet these standards. We are also pleased to recognize the significant contribution Thorndike Press is making in this important and growing field.

Lorraine H. Marchi, L.H.D.
Founder/CEO
NAVH

* Thorndike Press encompasses the following imprints: Thorndike, Wheeler, Walker and Large Print Press.

1

"I'd rather not go up and rehearse in the choir loft tonight, and I'd like you to humor me." With that request, Estelle Livett crossed her ample arms across her extremely ample bosom. Everyone in the Eternal Hope choir understood that, some days, their temperamental soprano just didn't feel like climbing the stairs.

Gracie Parks, substitute choir director, sighed. She knew from long experience that when Estelle was in one of her moods, an immovable object was thereby created. "But you can hear the resonance better from up there."

Amy Cantrell, the choir's youngest member, quietly concurred. "Come on, Estelle," she urged gently.

Lester Twomley added his two cents. "I myself wouldn't mind staying down here, Gracie."

Gracie understood why Lester might prefer sitting where they were to their usual position in the loft. His place was directly behind Estelle's. A small man, he couldn't help but be eclipsed by her bulk. Thus, while the Sunday churchgoers might sense that somewhere behind Estelle a tenor sang, there was no way they could confirm it with an actual sighting. Where he was now, Lester could at least see the director.

Gracie looked from face to face. "Very well. Let's rehearse, just for this evening, down here. Barb will be displeased, but that's the way it goes."

Estelle snorted. "Barb can just come to choir practice if she wants to do things her way."

Marge Lawrence, her hair arranged in an updo this evening and her music in her lap, looked at Gracie. "Do you know why she isn't here? Barb, I mean."

"All this rain has brought on a sinus attack. I told you, she feels wretched."

Amy slowly shook her head. "It's just been a steady downpour. Do you suppose we'll get even more?"

Don Delano stretched past Lester to pat her shoulder. "I looked at the weather service map before I came. There's a high pressure system moving in behind this swarm of storms. The weather should be fair tomorrow."

Gracie didn't trust the weather service as much as Don seemed to: the success of its usual guess rate was way too low. But if anyone knew how to read a weather map, Don did. As a high school science teacher, he often set his students meteorological projects.

She glanced out the window yet again. All afternoon the weather had been howling, wild and windy, as late spring thunderstorms marched across the area one behind the other. She could see no let-up in sight.

Like flashbulbs at a grand opening, brilliance flared across the clouds. The thunder followed closely. Gracie thought briefly of her cat Gooseberry, who disliked electrical storms.

But back to business. " 'Cantata 63' that Barb introduced last week. Let's start with the coda. As I recall, that was pretty shaky."

Music sheets rustled.

Gracie raised her baton.

Splack! Lightning struck. Instantly, the sanctuary snapped from brightness to deep gloom. Gracie squinted at her sheet music. The notes faded and blurred, especially the half-notes.

She frowned at the assembled singers.

"Now what? Should we wait, or sing in the dark, or go home?"

"None of the above." Lester Twomley, always the problem solver, hopped up and hastened through the door behind the altar. In moments he came trotting out with candles. Of course. Why let a little celestial mayhem interrupt practice? Moments later the choir was bathed in the quiet glow of candlelight.

Gracie raised her baton.

She lowered it. "Estelle, for pity's sake. Wait for my cue."

Estelle protested, "But I didn't start to sing yet!"

"Sounds like a siren." Dan frowned. "Yep. Siren out there. Maybe the lightning struck a building and it's a fire."

Gracie raised her baton.

Clup-clup-clup-clup . . .

She lowered the baton. She recognized the sound. Her Uncle Miltie had come through the front doors and was barreling up the aisle as fast as his walker would bring him. He was so excited he was nearly in front of it — and he was calling out something.

"Tornado! Take cover!" As soon as Gracie realized what he was saying, her brain froze in neutral. A . . . a. . . . Confusion leaped in and seized her senses.

Don yelled, "To the basement!" He gestured at Gracie and the others.

Her first reaction was one she had no time to utter. *But the basement stairs are at the other end of the building!* she thought to herself.

Tish Ball called, "Brace yourself in the doorway!"

"No, no, no!" Estelle shrieked. "That's for earthquakes!"

Then Don Delano's clear and booming baritone roared, "Under the pews! *Now!*"

Because they could all hear a freight train coming, a very noisy and frightening freight train.

But there was no railroad track at this end of Willow Bend.

2

The silence startled her. Everything, inside and out, was so very, very quiet. Cautiously, Gracie crept out from beneath the pew. She found no debris, no dust or bits of anything. That was odd. In all the news footage she had ever seen of tornado damage, debris covered everything.

She looked up. The ceiling appeared to have weathered whatever that was just fine. It sure had sounded, though, like the building was being torn apart. The lovely flow-green glass windows? All intact, thankfully, yet she had distinctly heard glass shatter.

Behind her, Estelle broke the silence, breathing heavily as she hauled herself from beneath the pew. How in the world had she fit there? Gracie saw her fellow choir members guiltily having the same thought.

"It's so quiet! Is everyone all right?" Marge struggled to her feet. And then voice after voice assured the world that all was well, as the frightening silence was dispelled.

Marge began to chatter inanely about the blessing of such an escape from death. But though Estelle immediately tried to organize everyone into search parties to check out damage, no one seemed to want to be organized at the moment.

Gracie headed for the tall front doors, for Uncle Miltie was already hurrying back outside. She left the sanctuary right behind him.

They stepped out into a golden, early evening half-light serenely stretching into the horizon. Had it not been for the ominous cloudbank to the northeast and the rainwater rushing down the street gutter, one would have doubted the proximity of a terrifying howling storm.

Uncle Miltie looked up and about. "Closest I ever came to one," was his only comment. He seemed lost in thought.

Gracie wrapped an arm around his shoulder. In the distance, sirens began to wail. Fire equipment and ambulances. Somewhere, there were people not nearly so lucky as the choir of Eternal Hope Church had been.

Uncle Miltie snapped out of his reverie. With mock grumpiness, he broke the ten-sion by snarling, "Someone owes me! I ripped both rubber tips off my walker, getting away from that stupid tornado."

Gracie laughed. "Whoever it is, what makes you think they're going to pay up?"

And then, suddenly, she gasped. As if on cue, a ten-dollar bill had tumbled out of the sky, landing at Uncle Miltie's feet. They stared at each other, stunned. How . . . ? What . . . ? Gracie began to say something, and Uncle Miltie might have too, had not his mouth been wide open. For now came another bill, this one a five. More fives. A fifty! They stared at one another.

From behind them, Marge cried out, "Look! Money! Pennies from heaven!"

"Pennies?! Twenties!" And the octogenarian Uncle Miltie watched in amazement as Estelle went one direction and Rick Harding in another, snatching bills out of the grass. Marge and Amy ran down the street, grabbing at the ground. Tish Ball and Tyne Anderson, the Turner twins, were smoothing out the bills they handed to one another.

Don and Lester, however, weren't laughing. They were strolling slowly, sadly, around the far corner of the church, staring up behind the steeple, followed by

14

Marybeth Bower, Bert Benton and the other choir members.

Curiosity got the better of Gracie, as it always was wont to do. She hurried over to join them.

She didn't have to ask what they were looking at. "Oh, my. Oh, no!" *Oh, dear God, why did You let this happen?*

A yew and two cherry trees lay uprooted in the side yard. As if leaving a little parting favor, the twister had spared the sanctuary windows while taking out every piece of glass in the back of the building. Gracie said a quick thank-you just to show that she noticed.

But the roof. Oh, the roof! That was a very different story! The shingles had been stripped off the whole southwest side of the building. Ten feet of roof decking, too, had been ripped away. Splintered rafter stubs protruded. The wound in the little church gaped, all sad and ragged, its innards exposed to the elements.

Don pointed. "It took out some upstairs windows. Do you see where they are?"

"No." Gracie gasped. "But, Don! If we had been up in the loft where we were supposed to be. . . ."

He finished her thought for her. "We can thank Estelle — and the good Lord who watches over us — we weren't!"

Les spoke up. "Do we have any tarps big enough?"

"I doubt it." Don's voice was heavy with sadness. "I'll run over to the lumber yard and pick up a few rolls. We can jury-rig something."

"Good. We really ought to cover it tonight, just in case of more rain. Wouldn't want the ceiling to sag and cave in." Lester gave the exposed area one last glance. "I'll go call the wardens and Pastor Paul. Anyone else?"

"That rental place on the highway. We'll need floodlights and a cherry picker," Rick added, poking his foot at a loose roofing shingle in the grass.

Lester headed off to do his duty.

Out on the street, tires squealed as a little black automobile pulled in against the curb and stopped. Gracie paused to watch one of her friends step out. His thick shock of salt-and-pepper hair glinted in the evening sun.

A sport-utility vehicle pulled in behind Rocky Gravino's car, dwarfing it. Ben Tomlinson, the *Mason County Gazette*'s photographer, leaped out. He dragged a big shoulder bag off the seat beside him and came running across the church yard, twisting knobs on a small camera.

Gracie's adored husband, the late Elmo Parks, had always referred to newsmen as too willing to descend instantly upon the latest survivors of any mishap. But Gracie had every respect for her dear friend and frequent co-conspirator, newspaper editor Rocco Gravino — even if she couldn't argue that here a tornado had touched down and, instantly, here too was Rocky also touching down, so to speak.

"Good evening, Rocky." Gracie had not realized until just now how heavy her voice sounded or how heavy the world weighed.

Rocky stopped beside her, but he didn't really see her. He was gazing past her toward the church roof. Ben hurried on by at a run and started shooting.

Don joined them. "H'lo, Rock. Don't happen to have a tape measure, do you?"

Rocky studied the church roof. "Your hole there is twenty-two feet across by about twelve feet high. I'd use three rolls and patch it double thick. Run the plastic right up over the ridge."

Don was impressed. "Since when do newspaper editors measure by eye?"

"Since fifty years, at least, when they had to be able to estimate newsprint rolls. So it really was a twister, hey?"

Naturally the men, true to the habits of their gender, immediately fell to talking about the prospective repairs, the cost, the method and technique, the size of the nails to be used, the advantages and disadvantages of thirty-pound tarpaper as opposed to twenty-pound stock, and whether the driver making the delivery from the building supply yard would be able to deliver the shingle packs directly onto the roof, as steep as it was.

At that moment Lester returned, announcing that a cherry picker and floodlights would be there in an hour. He, Gracie and the others stood around with Rocky and Don then, talking quietly.

By the time Pastor Paul Meyer arrived, a white media van was pulling up onto the grass, its roof filled with antennas and a white satellite dish.

Why am I standing here? Gracie wondered to herself. There was nothing she could do. Her best option was undoubtedly to go home, make a cup of tea and try to calm her frazzled nerves.

"How much money rained down from heaven?" Gracie asked her uncle. She still wasn't quite used to seeing him with the mustache he'd recently decided to grow.

"Don't know. Chief Bower confiscated

all the cash people picked up. Said it *must* belong to someone."

"Not a bad guess. Did he give you a receipt?"

"Better believe it. If nobody claims it, we get it back."

Gracie smiled. "Maybe they'll pay for those rubber tips you need. How much was it?"

"I didn't find as much as most folks, and I picked up eight hundred and thirty-seven dollars." Uncle Miltie snorted through his new mustache. "More than was called for — rubber walker tips are only two-ninety-five — but I could find a use for the extra."

Just then Pastor Paul's conversation with Rocky became audible. The minister's voice sounded unhappy. "As you know, Rocky, the church generates barely enough income to keep up with basic repairs, let alone emergencies."

"Insurance?"

"Yes, of course, but in order to afford any insurance at all, we had to opt for a large deductible."

Rocky shook his head. "There's a lot of structural damage up there, Paul."

"A lot. Even with an insurance claim, I doubt we can afford repair. This twister —"

Rocky interrupted. "I point out that it

was, legally speaking, an act of God."

Paul grimaced. "An act of God. What it is, Rocky, is a major financial crisis. It could sink this church."

3

It was nearly dark, but the memory of the storm's violence did not fade a bit with the waning day. Gracie wanted most of all to soak in a warm bath and then curl up in her soft, safe bed. *But is it safe? Is anywhere safe?* She shuddered.

Besides, too much was still going on here at the church. Rocky's local team covering the scene had now been supplemented by half a dozen big-city folk with well-coiffed hair and satellite feeds.

Gracie watched from the sidewalk as a perfectly manicured young blonde woman interviewed Pastor Paul. Behind them, floodlights illuminated the church's damaged roof. Half a dozen men from the congregation, on ladders and in the rented cherry picker, worked to secure a plastic tarp over the hole. It was all quite dramatic, really.

She looked at the man beside her. "Rocky, you were a big-city editor for years. Doesn't this make you want to jump back into the thick of it?"

He looked at her affectionately. "You mean like the old war horse pawing the ground when he hears the trumpet? No. What you're looking at right there is why I'm with the *Mason County Gazette*. When I was a youngster, the news was all-important. If your necktie was on crooked, it meant you were in such a big hurry to get the facts that you didn't care how you looked. Now, if you don't look good on TV, you're not a news reporter."

Looming at Gracie's left elbow, Police Chief Herb Bower nodded. "I hear you. I hate it when one of those news kids collars me for an interview, trying to look good while asking stupid questions."

The tall and burly Herb was one of the few people of Gracie's acquaintance who not only loomed standing up but could also loom sitting down. Gracie always felt a bit timid in his presence. The fact that he was a foot taller than her five-four and outweighed her by a hundred pounds may have had something to do with it. He asked Rocky, "Are you going to report it yourself?"

"I'm getting help with the lead articles but I'll toss in the editorial, then do the in-depth by myself tomorrow. Any police angle I should be pursuing?"

"I'll write the twister up for vandalism. Other than that, no," he joked.

Rocky cocked an eyebrow. "Nothing yet on the 'pennies' that fell from heaven?"

"Haven't had a chance to investigate what could have caused it. It was enough that I got the bills confiscated until we do know."

Pastor Paul's fifteen minutes of television fame were over. The fashionably attired reporter stood in front of the camera doing some sort of wrap-up. The leader of Gracie's flock made a hasty exit toward friendlier faces.

Rocky remarked as he joined them, "You look all in, Pastor. Should I offer you a restorative drink?"

"My tongue cleaveth to my mouth, but not from thirst," Paul answered, frazzled. "From keeping it from saying what I wanted to. Anyway, no matter *what* I say, it will wind up at less than a minute on air once they've edited it."

"What did you *want* to say?" Rocky was curious.

Gracie had come to know that Rocky's questions almost always prompted revelations, replies that usually gave away more than the interviewee wanted to say. It was simply a gift he had, and a handy one for a newspaperman.

"Well," Paul watched the repair work a moment, "what would *your* response be to, 'And how do you *feel* about this catastrophe, Pastor?' "

"My response would be, 'You can mail your donations, folks, to Eternal Hope Church at Box XYZ, Willow Bend, zip code, etc.' What? *Didn't* you play the sympathy chord?"

Herb drew a deep breath and broke in. "I'd like to look around inside, upstairs at the damage site, Pastor. Do I have your permission?"

Pastor Paul may have been born in the middle of the night, Gracie mused, but it wasn't last night. "I'm fine with that, so long as you tell me in advance what you're looking for." He certainly looked like a man with nothing to hide.

Herb pursed his lips a moment. What was he thinking? "The source of at least twenty-eight thousand dollars that seems just to have dropped out of the sky. I assume you know all the nooks and crannies up there if anyone does."

"If this church had a stash of twenty-eight thousand dollars tucked away, we'd be buying better insurance." Pastor Paul nodded toward Gracie. "Actually, though, I don't know the place nearly as well as Gracie here. I've only been here a few years."

Herb looked at her. "Come along?"

"I'm not about to stay behind!"

Thank you, Lord! Her beloved El had often chided her affectionately about her vivid curiosity. In fact, the whole family, blood relatives and in-laws, shared a sharper-than-average native nosiness. At the back of her mind she had even been rehearsing ways to get included, and here the Lord had just done it for her!

The four of them strolled across the lawn and in through the big front doors. *Why is Rocky?* Gracie wondered, and then she answered her own question. *Because nobody told him he couldn't, and he has a matchless instinct for a good story, which this surely promises to be.*

The power to the church was still out. Had the twister ripped out the line, or was it simply that the original loss had not yet been repaired? They clattered up the rickety old back stairs in the light of Chief Bower's powerful flashlight.

He stood at the rear of the choir loft and ran the light beam around the area. Gracie's breath caught. The two windows had shattered; glass shards lay across the choir seats. Broken glass lodged in the music stands. It twinkled in the light.

Pastor Paul closed his eyes. "My Lord God, I thank You right now that You spared our faithful choir. I praise Your name! Amen."

"Amen!" Gracie echoed him. She was one of those faithful spared. In fact, had she been standing on the little podium when it struck, someone right now would be picking glass out of her face and probably her eyes as well.

"What's in there?" Herb shone his light on a closet door.

"Hymnals," Gracie replied. "We replaced our congregational hymnbooks a few years ago and stored the old ones in there."

Paul frowned. "Why didn't they just dispose of them?"

"No one could bear to. They'd been our songbooks for over twenty years. So in the interest of harmony, the board just put them aside."

Herb shook the door. "Locked."

"I don't have a key to it." Paul looked at Gracie. "Do you?"

"You don't need one." Gracie could spend time explaining what Herb ought to do, or she could simply do it. She crossed to the closet, gripped the doorknob and pulled as she kicked the door just below the middle. It jerked open.

Herb rummaged briefly through the stacks of books and flashed his light into all the corners. He stepped back. "Any trick to closing it?"

"Just slam it."

Wham! It shut.

He continued his search of the area. He paused at the two-foot-high door to a little cubbyhole against the outside wall under the eaves. "What about this one?" He shone the beam at it.

"I have no idea. I never looked."

He wrenched it open with difficulty. Most of it had disappeared along with the shattered roof. He looked around inside it briefly and whistled.

Gracie was close enough to see.

Cash — ordinary, negotiable, always-welcome cash — thickly littered the floor of the little space.

4

Pastor Paul stood staring, aghast.

Chief Bower whipped out his cell phone. "Gladys. I'm upstairs at Eternal Hope Church. Send Jimmy over here now. I mean right now. And call the state liaison. I'd like a full fur-and-fiber team up here pronto."

Rocky came to his own conclusions. "You're acting like it's hot."

Herb glanced quickly at Pastor Paul. "I trust it isn't the weekly offering being held until the bank opens."

Pastor Paul shook his head emphatically.

Herb studied him carefully, then told all three of his companions, "Okay, folks, we're going to exit the way we entered, straight back to the stairs." He pointed. "We don't want to add any more evidence of human presence than is already here. Maybe even who uses that little cubby-hole." Again, he glanced at Pastor Paul.

Gracie led the way and jogged down the stairs in the dark. She had negotiated them thousands of times. Herb's flashlight beam tried unsuccessfully to keep ahead of her.

They stepped outside into the glare of the floodlights. A police car with full lights and siren came roaring to the curb, and Officer Jim Thompson leaped out with a big yellow roll of *POLICE LINE DO NOT CROSS* tape.

Herb turned to Pastor Paul. "Give a little more thought to some possible origins of that money, Paul. It's the kind of mystery I don't like."

"But . . . I don't . . . uh . . ."

"Good night, all." And Herb walked off to give instructions to Officer Thompson.

Gracie stood open-mouthed, as well. At least she hadn't been rendered totally speechless. "What's a 'foreign fiber' team?"

"Fur and fiber. Slang for a police lab crew that goes over the place looking for microscopic evidence like hairs, fabric fibers, fingerprints, that stuff."

"What's going to happen, Rocky? What is he thinking?"

Rocky shrugged. "I'm not placing any bets. You have to admit, it's just a mite unusual to uncover that much cash in a church closet."

"It's getting late, but I'm not the least bit sleepy. How about ice cream at my house,

29

the two of you?" Gracie suggested. "We have French vanilla, which is your basic rich vanilla, and Peanut Butter Cup. That's peanut butter flavor with chocolate morsels in it."

Pastor Paul, a bachelor of thirty, was grateful for the distraction. "I'd love it," he told Gracie.

Rocky bobbed his head. "Paul, why don't you drive over with me? I'll drop you off here when we leave."

Gracie led the two-car convoy to her house and pulled into her driveway.

Uncle Miltie, who'd gotten a ride home from the church earlier, was sitting on the front porch in the dark, rocking back and forth in the glider. "Couldn't sleep."

"I don't blame you. Coming in? Ice cream?" She paused and turned to Rocky and her minister. "It's so mild, let's have it out here. Orders?"

They all wanted Peanut Butter Cup. While the men settled themselves on the porch, she hurried in to scoop ice cream.

She was so flustered by events of the extraordinary evening that she almost forgot to add a dash of whipped cream and the maraschino cherries.

Paul had apparently recovered his senses. As she brought out the ice cream, carrying it on her old tray, he was trying to figure out some explanation for what he'd seen. "I tell you, that's the last place in the world I would expect to find a dime, let alone . . . I mean, I still can't believe it."

"Believe it." Uncle Miltie accepted a dish of ice cream and a napkin.

Paul was almost too distracted to notice what he was spooning into his mouth. "It could have been lying up there for years and years. We may have been sitting on a fortune for decades."

Rocky shook his head. "They're the new bills. The redesigned twenties, fives and tens with off-center portraits. Current issue. Thank you, Gracie. You know what this means, Paul. Someone in your Eternal Hope congregation has a lot of explaining to do. Most logically, even, it has to be a member of the choir. They're up there anytime. Carrying packages up and down. Whatever. Heaving wheelbarrows up and down. There's enough money up there, someone *had* to use a wheelbarrow. Why would anyone question it?"

"I question it! I mean, I question your whole premise." Gracie sat down with the last dish, her own, and propped the tray against her chair. "If someone were tucking things away up there, we'd know it.

31

Pat would know it." She meant Pat Allen, the church secretary.

"And you better bet Herb is going to ride her hard on that one. He'll question her six ways from Sunday."

"Gracie's right," Uncle Miltie added. "Someone would notice. She was tactful enough that she didn't say it exactly, but most of the people in that church are busybodies, anyway. Straight from the get-go."

"Uncle Miltie!" Gracie chided.

Paul smiled. "He has a point, however baldly stated. And just about anyone could get in there."

"Okay," Rocky pressed, "so who has a key? Gracie? I know you do."

"But I don't know who else."

Paul shook his head. "I don't know either. Pat will know." He added, for Rocky's sake, "Pat assigns the keys. I'm certain she keeps a list. But I think, for starters, I'd say, 'the world.' Everyone in the choir, everyone on the board, and everyone associated with our Christian ed program. Also anyone who regularly works in the kitchen — and the cleaning people, don't forget."

Had he left out any major groups? Gracie couldn't say. But then, her brain was still a muddle, and she was starting, finally, to feel tired.

Rocky paused, his major attention still on the ice cream rather than the conversation. "Let's say that leaves five people left in town without a key. Six; I don't have one. So how would they break in?"

Uncle Miltie wrinkled his nose. "Break into a church? That makes me think of the reason prisoners eat strawberries — to break out!"

Uncle Miltie enjoyed his joke and Rocky went back to the ice cream. "This is very good ice cream, Gracie." Rocky savored it a moment. "What safer place to store booty than a church attic? No one's ever going to suspect, and no one ever goes up there. You've got the place to yourself."

"Whether you're a church member or not, since a lot of nonmembers actually go in and out." Gracie thought a moment. "I suppose anyone with a table knife or a pair of kindergarten scissors could break in. The locks on the downstairs doors are in about the same state as that closet lock we shook open tonight."

"Who," Rocky asked, "goes in and out who's not a member?"

"The cleaning crew," Paul said. "They're hired from outside. Repairmen — that old building is practically falling down. It sees a lot of them, even without the twister's

help. And anyone who is seeking temporary aid. We have a food bank, for in-
stance."

Rocky stared. "You're telling me you let
them have the run of the place?"

Uncle Miltie scraped his dish. "That's
what churches are for, and, besides, who's
going to steal from Eternal Hope? And
what's to steal? The only money there is in
the secretary's office, and she keeps very
little on hand."

Paul nodded emphatically. "We don't
even have a safe."

"You don't need one." Rocky set his dish
aside. "You've got the choir loft."

5

Twelve hours since twister. Gracie had not slept at all well. She wondered how Uncle Miltie had fared — or poor Paul Meyer, for that matter. She was almost tempted to rap at Uncle Miltie's door, but she did not. If he had not slept as soundly as he usually did, he ought not be awakened yet.

She munched her cereal in blessed silence. *Thank You, Lord, for a respite, however temporary, from the noise of the morning TV news!*

Marge appeared beyond the screen at the back door. With a cheery smile, she looked in curiously, then opened the door.

Gracie told her, "You're here early. I doubt Pat will be there yet." Just before she had gone to bed, Gracie had phoned Marge to plan a visit together to the church office. They had been due to help out with filing and other paperwork.

"Coffee?" Marge swept on past and over to the pot. She answered her own question by pouring a cup. "Church secretaries are very efficient. They have to be. You know that." Marge plunked herself down at the table. "She's usually in at eight. I'm betting she shows up earlier today, what with all the fallout and confusion from the storm."

"True. She has her work cut out for her. That's why I phoned."

Marge looked worried. "One of her tasks might be keeping Pastor Paul out of jail. Do you realize that? I'm sure Herb suspects him, especially since he's only been at Eternal Hope for three years."

"He suspects *all* of us. I simply can't imagine anyone using that cubbyhole to salt away thousands of dollars. It's beyond comprehension."

Gooseberry meowed by Gracie's chair. She scooped him into her lap without thinking and mechanically stroked the orange and black fur. But, being a cat desirous of complete and utter attention, he looked up at her as he happily flexed his claws as his paws lay upon her leg.

"Ack! Gooseberry! That hurt!" He had her focused on him now.

Unperturbed, he blotted up the restored adulation, eyes half closed, chin extended, ribs vibrating. His purr sounded like a sports car with an inadequate muffler.

When the two friends left a few minutes

later, Uncle Miltie still had not risen. Gracie left a note on the refrigerator: *Gone to EH. Back by noon.*

Gracie pulled her old Cadillac, Fannie Mae, into the Eternal Hope parking lot and stopped. Nearly the whole area was now cordoned off!

Looking flustered and angry, Pat Allen, the secretary, had set up her office under the tulip tree just this side of the police tape. She sat in her accustomed secretarial chair behind a long folding table. It was covered by stacks of papers, the in- and out-baskets and her Rolodex. A cordless phone lay by her elbow.

She watched Gracie and Marge as they headed in her direction.

"What's going on?" Marge demanded.

"They are examining the office for evidence." Pat's voice was glacial. "When I insisted on doing my work, they let me partially set up here. Reluctantly, I might add. And if it starts to rain they can help me move all this inside, reluctant or not."

Gracie smiled slightly. "I do hope they don't try to sell you any tickets for the police raffle. You don't look in a mood to buy."

"Well, since they're assuming that the money is ill-gotten, the corollary is that therefore we all must be criminals. Unfortunately, I left the altar flowers book in the back of the church. When they hustled me out and set me up here this morning, I forgot to bring it. Now I need it. It's little inconveniences like that that irk so much."

"Where did you leave the book?" Gracie asked.

"On the counter in the back room above where the vases are kept. They sealed the back door somehow. I tried."

"Be right back." Gracie had noticed as a sort of point of curiosity that the yellow police tape stretched around only the front of the church. She walked around the back and tried her key in the door. Pat was right. Either the lock was changed, or the police had found some magical means of sealing it.

She went next to the window facing onto the back parking lot. She climbed up on the gardeners' hose box beside it and tried to raise it. It slid right open, just as it had for ten years, ever since the brass window lock broke off.

She slipped inside, pausing on the sill. She wanted to believe she was doing nothing illegal; she had a key to the church, after all. But she tried to maintain silence anyway, let sleeping dogs lie. She descended inside onto the countertop eighteen inches below the sill.

She didn't even have to touch the floor. The record book lay right there, exactly as Pat had described. Gracie tucked it under her arm and slipped back out. Once on the ground, she looked around to see that she'd disturbed nothing visibly and returned to Marge and Pat.

They seemed to be arguing about whether it was possible to sue the police for inconvenience caused. Gracie handed Pat her record book.

Pat brightened. "I'm not even going to ask. Thank you! I have a dozen entries that ought to be put in or caught up to date." Her brief cheer faded instantly. With a frown, she looked out across the parking lot.

Eyeing the police tape cautiously, one might even say fearfully, a slim young woman was crossing the lot toward them. Gracie's first thought was: *This is a woman in need of help, if ever there was!* In fact, that was her second thought as well.

With well-worn clothes and plain brown, shoulder-length hair in need of shampooing, she appeared badly used by the world. Her eyes had dark rings under them. "I'm looking for the pastor, please."

"I'm afraid he's in a meeting."

The woman looked confused, and very weary. "When can I talk to him?"

"Leave a number and he'll call you as soon as he's free."

"I don't have a phone."

"Your address?"

"We're, uh, just passing through and I don't have one. Yet."

"Car license?"

"I'm sorry. My husband has the car and he's out of town. I don't remember the number. Look. I'll, uh, just go over there and wait until these other women are, uh, done with their, uh, business."

Pat shook her head. "They came to help me with some paperwork. Obviously, that's not going to happen in the near future. Perhaps I can assist you now?"

The young woman licked her lips. Then she blurted, "My husband is missing. He's a handyman. He's very good. I don't have a job so there's no money coming in and my children need food. And Bradley — he's my younger son — is sick." She had a strong Southern accent of some sort.

"We have a food bank, but it's not accessible now." Pat nodded toward the front door. "Can you come back this afternoon? They should be done in there by then and

40

we can all get back inside. Also, our pastor will be free then and he can set you up with help."

"Yes." The young woman looked again toward the church. She nodded. "Yes, that will be okay. Yes."

"We'll try to tend to your needs then!" Pat assured her.

The woman smiled tentatively back and turned away.

Marge looked at Gracie. Gracie looked at Marge.

"Wait!" Waving a hasty good-bye to Pat, Gracie jogged to catch up. "Do you need food right now?"

"Yes." The woman looked nervous. "But, uh, this afternoon will be fine. It's, uh, all right, really."

Very gently — so gently the woman surely didn't know what was happening — Gracie shouldered her toward Fannie Mae. "What's your name?"

"Hannah. Uh, Hannah Cates."

Gracie fell in at the woman's other elbow. "And you were born where?"

"Arkansas." The woman grinned wanly. "Thought you'd know, from my accent."

"You sound Southern and cultured. That's all I could tell. Marge and I do catering sometimes. After we helped Pat, we were going to go out to lunch and then purchase some staples we need."

"And so," Marge completed the thought, "why don't you come along with us? We'll buy the food on our list and also some for you, and then take you to lunch with us. By then Pastor Paul will probably be available."

Hannah stopped in her tracks. "I can't. Thank you, but I'm very sorry. I couldn't let you do that!"

Gracie raised her voice just a tad. "Now, listen. We can make our usual food contribution to the church's closet and hand it to Pat, whom you talked to, and then she will hand it to you. Or we can simply hand it to you to start with and save Pat one more chore. Believe me. This will be easier."

"But I can't pay you back."

"It's not expected! We're going to go eat lunch, anyway. One more sandwich at Abe's deli won't make a bit of difference."

Hannah hesitated. How could she know that to waver the least bit was to lose an argument with Marge or Gracie, either one? In moments they had cajoled her into Fannie Mae. The three of them were on their way to the supermarket.

Yet Gracie couldn't help but wonder: In

what meeting had Paul been involved?
Nothing church-associated. She knew that
much. Could it have been, perchance, a
police interrogation?

6

Gracie pondered the effect of the hoisin sauce in this chicken dish. The taste and texture were both superb. She really ought to use such exotic and interesting sauces more in her own cooking. They added so much. On the other hand, Uncle Miltie tended to like certain things and turn up his nose at anything with a new or unusual (to him) flavor.

Across from her in the booth, Marge was finishing off her lunch. Celestial City, Willow Bend's Chinese restaurant, had been Marge's idea, and what a delicious and useful idea it was! The all-you-can-eat lunch buffet aspect worked very well for Hannah, while Marge and Gracie ordered from the menu and received, as always, more food than they could eat. Now they both had doggie bags to give Hannah when they parted.

Poor Hannah. She seemed to tackle the task of eating lunch with a pitiful excess of gusto. When had she last eaten well? Extremely reluctant to talk about herself, she answered mostly with yesses, nos and I-don't-knows.

The only information she volunteered, and she did so enthusiastically, was that her husband was an excellent young man with many admirable skills. It was only bad luck that had kept him from finding good work, and, no, he wasn't deliberately abandoning them. He was probably out of state on some pick-up job and for the moment out of touch with the whole world.

Neither Marge nor Gracie pressed the issue or pried. The purpose of this lunch had been to feed Hannah, not to glean information.

Conversation had lapsed. What topic should she introduce next? When Marge asked Hannah about her children, the young woman instantly was on her guard, responding cautiously and vaguely. All they could learn from her was what they already knew, that she had two sons. So Gracie had tried the subject of food next; Hannah did not apparently cook much. She had tried to draw out Hannah's interest in faith, if any. She had there drawn a blank, too. If Hannah trusted God, she didn't seem inclined to let anyone know.

Cats? No. Marge tried dogs. Also, no.

God, food and cats. *What else is there in life, Hannah? What enlivens your mind and lifts your spirits? What makes you tick, after all, poor child?*

When the bill arrived, Hannah offered neither to pay nor to get the tip. Gracie had expected they would treat her — as they had insisted she come with them — but it is usually considered polite, at least, to offer.

Hannah seemed nervous and ashamed while Gracie accepted Marge's share. Gracie longed to know more of what was going on inside this mysterious young woman's head and heart.

They then settled themselves into Fannie Mae and returned to the church.

Pat Allen was still holding court under her tree out by the church parking lot, with the yellow police tape still draped from bush to traffic cone to handrail to whatever else would support it. Inconvenience, in other words, still reigned supreme. No food bank today.

Her groceries and Chinese leftovers in hand, Hannah offered a muted good-bye and left.

Marge had an appointment to interview someone for a job at her gift shop. "On the phone, he sounded like a nice young man.

He's a neighbor of the Cantrells."

Gracie took her there and said, as she dropped her off at the front door, "Thanks for your part in the day, Marge. We did the right thing, giving her support . . . and lunch . . . and food to fall back on."

The sun had been skipping playfully among the clouds since noon. Now it broke forth in full glory. Gracie reached for her sunglasses. She groped around for them in her purse unsuccessfully.

Marge turned around and seeing her friend still there, came back to stick her head in the car window. "What?"

"My sunglasses."

"You were wearing them when you went into the restaurant."

"Mmm. Then I suspect they're still there." Gracie waved good-bye and drove back to Celestial City.

She addressed the slight, pretty woman beside the receptionist's dais. "When we were here for lunch, I may have left a pair of sunglasses at the table."

The woman waved her toward the dining room. Gracie then walked back to their table unescorted. A man was now seated where, twenty minutes ago, Marge had sat.

Her mouth dropped open. "Why, Pastor Paul! Good afternoon!" Gracie noted with interest that he was eating with chopsticks, and quite capably, too.

"Oh, hello, Gracie." He waved a hand absently. "Sit. Join me."

"I don't mean to intrude. I thought I might have left my sunglasses behind. We ate in this very booth an hour ago."

Reaching down beside him, he handed her her flowered sunglasses. "I thought they looked like yours. They're distinctive."

"El gave them to me years ago. I'd hate to lose them." Gracie was all set to leave. Heaven knows, she had a hundred things to do at home and the day over half gone already. Instead, she slipped into the booth across from him. "What's wrong?"

He sighed. "Nothing, really. I'm just worn out."

"Pat said you were in a meeting."

He sighed again. "Yes. A meeting in Herb's office. Two hours of answering questions. Then a break, and an hour and a half more."

"It's hard to imagine that Herb could think up that many."

"Not Herb. He wasn't even there. In town here, we now have two FBI agents, an agent from Alcohol, Tobacco and Firearms, and three — count 'em, three! —

Drug Enforcement Agency folk."

"Why?" The light suddenly dawned. "That money in the church! Of course!"

Paul nodded. "Those people are trained to think up hours and hours worth of questions. But there was only *one* question, really: 'Where did I get the money I stashed up there?' "

Gracie considered this a few moments. "Am I guessing correctly that they're not quite satisfied with your answers yet?"

"Excellent guess, especially since I only had one answer: 'I don't know.' "

A horrible thought popped into Gracie's head. "We have a board meeting tonight! Oh, dear. Do you want to cancel?"

"No. I'm going home and I am going to read for a while. I'll be fine by tonight. Besides, that twister gave us too much important business that can't wait."

"Wicked twister!" Gracie stood up.

"Indeed, indeed!" And a slight smile hovered for an instant on the pastor's face. "I'll see you this evening, Gracie. Blessings."

"Blessings." She left.

Yes. Blessings. We need blessings, Father, lots of them, to get through this confusing mess!

Lots and lots.

7

Considering how dejected Pastor Paul had looked at the restaurant in the afternoon, he had certainly snapped back well. He presided now over the emergency board meeting with his usual aplomb. He intoned the invocation and relinquished the meeting to Jessica Larson.

Jessica was soon asking their interim treasurer, Lester Twomley, to discuss an important aspect of this emergency session, the treasurer's report.

Lester cleared his throat. "As you know, our former treasurer, who was with us only a brief time, left the books in some disarray when he moved out of state. You will recall that at the last regular meeting, I noted several discrepancies. It turned out that in his arguments with the bank, the bank happened to be right after all. That resulted in fewer assets than we thought we had, particularly the account used for checking and disbursement."

Estelle Livett said, "Wait," and scrawled

hastily. She was apparently in charge of taking minutes tonight. She raised her eyes and nodded.

Lester continued. "The petty cash drawer was exhausted by our purchase of emergency repair materials for the hole in our roof. In fact, the supplies were more than the church had on hand, so Don and I covered the difference. We got repair estimates today from Roy Bell, Bill Ruff and Rocky Gravino. Then —"

"Wait," said Estelle again, but her voice was drowned out by Jessica's.

"Rocky Gravino!" Jessica erupted. "Why in the world would you entertain a construction bid from a newspaper editor?!"

"I didn't say bid, Jessica. An estimate. Calm down." With elaborate patience, Lester explained, "He is extremely knowledgeable about estimates and actual costs. You will remember that the *Mason County Gazette* building had that little problem with its roof a year or so ago. Also, he hears about and records many, many bids as part of the news-gathering process — virtually every public bid in the county. He knows the bid to build the gazebo in Fairweather Park, for example. And the fire damage repairs at the firehouse. We value his opinion in this matter."

Don Delano was not a board member, but he was sitting in on this session to offer some extra perspective, Gracie knew. "I worked for a construction crew while I was in grad school. Allowing for inflation over the last few years, the estimates we got are not out of line. This is about what it's going to cost us."

"It doesn't matter what the total is," Jessica reminded them. "Our insurance covers everything beyond the deductible."

"No," Pastor Paul said quietly, "it will not cover any of it."

Gracie wasn't sure if she'd heard him correctly. She glanced about. Everyone else looked just as startled.

"Lester was being too gracious," Paul said. "Our previous treasurer, Bill Smyth, didn't just leave the books in a mess. He left bills unpaid. One of them was the insurance."

"Rats! If he hadn't left the state on his own," Don complained, "we could chase him out. You know, like all those villagers with torches, running uphill to Frankenstein's castle."

Jessica glared at him. "This is no time for levity."

"Laugh or cry. Your choice." Don did not look in a jovial mood.

Gracie felt ready to cry.

Paul sighed. "We're here tonight to explore options. And I might as well say right up front, one of them is to close our doors."

Willow Bend's most popular mortgage banker, Frederick Baxter, must have come to the meeting directly from his office. He pulled his necktie knot loose with a sigh. "Lester, grab a marker there and put our assets up on the whiteboard."

Lester nodded grimly. He drew a vertical line down the center of the two-by-four-foot bulletin board from top to bottom. Then, referring to his notes, he sketched the cash on hand, the savings account, the two certificates of deposit, and the estimated donations based upon annual pledges. All that fit on one side with a bit of space to spare. On the other side he wrote the three estimates they had obtained so far. The figures on the two sides did not compare well.

Fred Baxter stood up and took off his jacket. "I can tell right now, this is going to be a long session."

Long session, indeed! At twenty after ten, Gracie felt about ready to melt down into a little puddle under the table.

Estelle still bravely carried on, writing feverishly and occasionally shouting, "Wait!"

Jessica was doing a fine job of keeping discussions on track and on topic.

But Pastor Paul seemed stunned, now, and no wonder. His beloved Eternal Hope Church was paused on the brink of destruction. Never before had it been challenged by a crisis of this magnitude, not even during the early days as its ministry was just becoming established. In fact, Gracie tried to think of any time at all when they had faced such massive expenditures with so few funds. She could remember none.

Lord, I don't like the way this is going! Please feel free to intrude here. Pastor Paul needs more than our support.

Finally, as the clock ticked ever closer toward the next day, Gracie asked the question to which she pretty well knew the answer already. "Do we have any resources whatever for our routine ministries?"

Please, God —

Pastor Paul answered, "No."

"We have people in need. The young woman who came today, Hannah —"

"No." Paul said softly, "It was very good of you and Marge to take her out for lunch today. But that sort of thing — one on one — is about all we'll be doing for a while."

"But be careful," Pat Allen warned. "There are a lot of scam artists out there, Gracie. I suspect you're too kindhearted to realize how many moochers try to take advantage of aid programs like ours. No one has ever seen her children. We have no idea whether a child even exists. It could be just another attempt by someone to wring money out of us that they don't deserve. You don't know. That happens a lot."

Lester smiled sadly. "A week ago, we were happily living in a fool's paradise. We thought we had thousands of dollars more than we actually do. Had anyone asked then, or even two days ago, we gladly would have helped them. But the entire petty cash fund, not to mention all the —" He waved a hand toward the whiteboard. "Well, there you have it."

"But helping people find God and get through life is what we're all about!" Gracie protested.

Paul replied, "We can't help anyone do anything if we don't exist."

All Gracie could think of to say was, "I request a full vote."

"Good idea." Pastor Paul looked expectantly at Jessica.

She frowned. "Does anyone move that we suspend current ministries and devote all our resources to repair?"

Lester looked straight at Gracie as he said, "I so move."

"Second." Fred Baxter reached for his suit coat.

"Moved and seconded. In favor? Opposed? Carried."

Now what? I'm so sorry, God.

And that was that. Gracie's had been the only opposing vote.

8

Gracie recalled, as she was waking up, how gloomy she had felt before going to bed, drained by that terrible board meeting. She still felt emptied, even after a night's sleep. Her dreams had bothered her greatly, but she suddenly couldn't remember what they were.

Rising, she went through the familiar rituals of preparing for the day. Her thoughts were certainly not on her activities (she mislaid the toothpaste tube cap not once but twice).

What do we do now, Lord? We have all our regulars — the people who depend upon us for help — and Hannah as well. How can we turn our backs? And yet, Paul has a point. We can't be there to help if we don't exist. I'm torn, Lord. Show the way, I beg You.

She walked downstairs and headed toward the sound of the television morning news. In the kitchen, Uncle Miltie hunkered over his big bowl of bran flakes, watching rapt as a neatly attired young woman stood in front of a pile of wreckage addressing the camera. A rumpled side of a house trailer lay among the rubble. The reporter said something about a tornado. Apparently another had touched down somewhere yesterday.

He had milk on his mustache, blending its white with his.

Two days ago, a different reporter had stood in front of the Eternal Hope Church saying similar things. How often had Gracie watched news items without grasping that these were real people hurting in oh-so-real ways? Real! Real had never before seemed quite so real to her. The wicked twister had done at least that much to awaken her.

Gooseberry rubbed against her legs. "Uncle Miltie? Did you feed the cat this morning?" Pause. "Uncle Miltie!"

"Huh?" Now his attention was focused on the histrionics of a salesman in a car lot.

She repeated loudly, "Did you feed Gooseberry?"

"Not lately."

Her beloved El had been fond of saying, "News is the same old thing happening to different people." He had stolen the line — from where she didn't know. Now the handsome young male anchor discussed the way new federal anti-crime funds were going to be spent, so much for drug interdiction, so much for gun control, so much for white-collar computer crimes, so much for, etc. But was Uncle Miltie actually absorbing all of this, becoming admirably well informed, or was it simply that he liked the noise and sense of connectedness to the world at large first thing in the morning?

She was reaching for the cat food when the doorbell rang. "Just a moment, Mr. Impatience."

Gooseberry followed closely on her heels as she walked out through the living room to answer the door. Obviously, the wily cat was not about to lose sight of the source of his breakfast.

Three men, each as immaculately groomed as that TV news reporter, stood on Gracie's front porch. All three sported white shirts, dark suits, and short hair cuts. She opened the door.

The tallest of them, a blond, bronzed young fellow, held out a badge case at easy viewing level. "Mrs. Grace Lynn Parks? We're from the Federal Bureau of Investigation and the Drug Enforcement Agency, ma'am. Martin Grzbovsky."

Gracie laid her fingers on his wrist a moment to prevent him from withdrawing the badge. She wanted to see it better. His I.D. card spelled his name Grzbovsky. She stepped back and smiled. "I'll bet you have a hard time ordering things by phone."

The rather short, chubby, middle-aged man laughed.

Mr. Grzbovsky frowned, looking confused. "Actually, I prefer purchasing online."

The chubby fellow extended his hand. "Milton Conley. With the DEA. How do you do, Mrs. Parks?"

And the third man, in age probably somewhere about halfway between his colleagues, nodded slightly. "FBI field supervisor Joseph Patterson."

She waved a hand. "Please come in, gentlemen. Be seated. May I bring you coffee or something?"

Each mumbled a no-thank-you and bade her sit as well. She chose her favorite chair and let them arrange themselves as they wished.

"What can I do for you gentlemen?"

Gooseberry hopped up into her lap, squirmed around and settled.

They began asking about a number of basic things, including a few questions that

Gracie could see no reason for. Mr. Conley did not ask much. She knew that all this was merely preliminary, and not the real reason they had come here. Unfortunately, she had not yet eaten breakfast. Finally, they started getting to the heart of the matter.

Mr. Grzbovsky asked, "How long have you known Paul Meyer?"

"Since he was called to our church a little over three years ago. A bit longer, even. I was on the pastoral search committee."

So had Elmo Parks been, and it was he who had touted him when others worried about his youth. *Look how Paul has grown since then, in favor with God and man, as the saying goes. He has fulfilled El's predictions and then some. El was such a wise man.*

Gooseberry sat up and reminded her that he, too, had not yet eaten.

"And in the choir."

"Yes." Gracie's tummy growled. She tried to see where their questioning might be headed. She could not. So far, they had asked nothing they did not probably already know. But then, she figured, investigators usually skated around the edge a while before heading for the middle.

"Ms. Parks, are you satisfied with your

61

religious experience at Eternal Hope Church?"

Gracie found herself beginning to feel irritated. She shouldn't let them bother her, but she couldn't help but resent that kind of question. "To answer you adequately would take more time than I wish to spare."

"Answer it anyway, please."

"Very well." She would have liked more time to frame her reply. "I don't know what you mean by satisfaction with some sort of religious experience. That has very little to do with faith. Pastor Paul's messages are well grounded and deep. In other words, we're well fed spiritually. But that is not exactly a religious experience any more than everyday meals are a culinary experience. But we — most of us, at least — attend not for what we get out of it but for what we give to God: corporate worship. In this sense, 'corporate' means 'the body of believers.' "

That obviously went right over Mr. Grzbovsky's head and probably the others' as well. Gracie didn't care. She was very hungry. Gooseberry stuffed his face up under her chin, prodding her.

Gracie heard the kitchen television set go quiet abruptly. Uncle Miltie, that lucky fellow, was done with *his* breakfast.

"On a scale of one to ten," Mr. Grzbovsky continued undeterred, "how would you rate the quality of your religious experience at Eternal Hope Church?"

She sighed. "Mr. Grzbovsky, Mr. Patterson, Mr. Conley. Will you please simply ask what you want to know instead of going through all these preliminaries?"

Mr. Conley stared at her impassively. "Ms. Parks, yesterday, you and Margery Lawrence met a woman named Hannah Cates at the church. The three of you went out to lunch together. You apparently discussed a number of topics. When you three returned to the church, Ms. Cates carried away two plastic grocery bags and boxes with unknown contents. Immediately —"

"Fried rice, beef and broccoli stir-fry, almond chicken and noodles. Now you know the contents of the boxes."

"Immediately after dropping Ms. Cates off at the church, you took Ms. Lawrence downtown and let her out. Then you returned alone to the restaurant to meet Paul Meyer. For what purpose, Ms. Parks? What did you discuss?"

"To meet —" She felt her mouth drop open. "But we —" And her irritation turned into just plain anger. *You people were*

63

following us! You probably are following all of us! As if you had nothing better to do!

Very well. She would be boringly truthful. "My sunglasses."

"What?"

"We discussed my sunglasses, which I inadvertently had left at the restaurant. I really can't see that this time is being spent fruitfully."

"Ms. Parks, you do not seem to realize that you and your fellow church members are the prime suspects in an ongoing investigation. You are —"

"Investigation of what crime? This is all about that money in the choir loft, right? Gentlemen, possessing money is not a crime, although we get penalized for it anyway every April fifteenth. Until, and unless, you can identify some crime, we are not suspects."

"Very well, you are people of interest."

"Are you familiar with scripture, Mr. Patterson?"

"Yes, I am. I —"

"Good! Then I need not quote chapter and verse in Titus. There, the apostle Paul claims that to the innocent, everything is pure — that is, innocent. But the wicked cannot see purity anywhere. When you call law-abiding citizens suspects, it says far more about you than it does about us."

Mr. Conley quickly spoke, attempting to smooth the ruffled feathers on both sides of the conversation. "It is our experience, Ms. Parks, that when you have a lot of unmarked bills in one place, *something* crooked is going on. We —"

Gracie now was incredibly hungry. "I can show you three people that I know of in this town — all of them over seventy — who have mattresses stuffed with money. Some of it is left over from the Y2K scare. Others simply don't trust banks. Thousands of dollars in unmarked bills, and not a cent of it illegally obtained."

Gooseberry propelled himself to standing position and pushed off onto the floor. He strolled toward the kitchen. Perhaps Uncle Miltie would take pity on him.

Mr. Patterson continued. "Let's talk about your involvement in the church. You have been a member of the church board for how long?"

"I don't recall. I suppose six or seven years."

No, Gooseberry was not going to find relief in Uncle Miltie. Here came the man, his cap already on his head, his walker clunking through the room. "S'cuse me, folks," was all he said. He clumped out the front door. Gracie listened to him negotiate the front steps and continue out of earshot.

Mr. Grzbovsky was saying, "Our records show you've been a board member for nine."

"I had no idea you kept records on that." Gracie's attention returned to the moment.

Mr. Patterson let the slightest of smirks show on his otherwise passive face. "I would think you would keep careful records, Ms. Parks. After all, every plus mark serves to help balance the black ones when you stand in judgment. You are going to be judged, aren't you?"

That did it. Gracie twisted a bit in her chair to face him squarely. "Mr. Patterson. When I face my Lord in judgment, the black marks that will be held against me will be only those which I knew about but for which I failed to ask His forgiveness. And my failure to ask forgiveness will itself be one of them. He forgets the forgiven sins. He said so."

"But you surely want to get into heaven. Therefore —"

"My only claim for entrance into heaven will be the blood of Jesus, which pays my way. That alone. Not deeds, not even correct behavior. And certainly not a checklist of plus marks."

The phone rang at her elbow. She jumped, took a deep breath to settle her jangling nerves, and answered it. She passed it across to Mr. Grzbovsky. "It's for you."

He spoke into it a few moments, thanked the caller and hung up. "Ms. Parks, we are grateful for your time. We may have other questions, so please don't leave town." He stood up.

The other two rose.

Gracie gratefully stood up. She ushered them to the door. "God bless your day, gentlemen."

They left. And as she was closing the door, she heard Mr. Grzbovsky say, "They've just picked up that Hannah Cates. Let's go talk to her."

9

Pastor Paul stuck his head in the door of the vesting room and asked, "Did anyone in here ever hear of someone named Harold Mayhew? Can you let me know after the service?"

The choir was suiting up for the second service. Pastor Paul left, closing the door behind him.

"Wait." Marge paused from adjusting her robe. Her hair was done up in charming ringlets today, none of them quite long enough to touch the shoulders of her vestment. "I'm thinking."

Gracie picked up her music folder. She was ready.

"Mayhew. Mayhew." Estelle Livett tipped her head. "I knew that name was familiar! He works for the town. A custodian, I believe. He's been at the municipal building ever since I can remember."

From her El's days in local politics, Gracie dredged up the memory of a Harold. She had never heard his last name.

Barb burst in through the door. "Hurry! Let's get up there, people! Hurry!"

Gracie followed Rick Harding up the rickety old stairs into the choir loft. She paused, gasping, at the place where that cubbyhole, a few days ago, had hidden a fortune. The whole hole was gone now. The door had been taken out and the paneling between it and the loft stripped away. Only the ancient studs were left. No doubt agents of some overzealous branch of the federal government were responsible for its removal.

Above and behind the assembling choir, rain clattered on the plastic-sheet patch over their church's wounded roof. Wind rattled it. A lonely plastic bucket immediately behind Rick's chair caught the one persistent drip that had always landed there.

Barb signaled "Rise." The choir rose.

This morning they were opening with "The Maker of Sun and Moon," a lovely piece they hardly ever used. Gracie noted that the melody was harmonized by Ralph Vaughan Williams, and she wondered idly, as she always did, why his first name was always pronounced Rafe, long *a*, when anyone else would be plain old Ralph with short *a* and the *l* intact.

The organ crescendo ushered in the final verse. *O perfect love . . . O light beyond our ken.* Yes! God both is and does all of that! So what was He going to do about this church's financial morass? And what about that cash that so lately had lain directly behind Gracie as she sang His praise? What a confusing thing is life!

The service unfolding this morning resembled quite plausibly the usual worship in the usual sequence. One might never know that calamity loomed. Gracie welcomed the routine of it.

Sermon time. Pastor Paul stepped away from the lectern. "I am dispensing with the usual sermon today. Instead, I must tell you where we stand financially."

And he did so. He minced no words. He did no whitewashing. And he talked about the lapse of the insurance policy.

The congregation sat in silence, as dismayed as the board had been.

"These are our options." He recited them. They were not many.

"Now to quell rumors."

Gracie listened more carefully. What rumors? No doubt the pastor heard a lot of them.

"The first is the sum of money found up behind the choir loft. I've heard all sorts of wild guesses about the amount." Pastor Paul looked around. "The official total is just short of ninety thousand dollars. We have no idea how it got there."

As he said that, Gracie realized for the first time how ridiculous that claim might sound to an outsider's ear. Nearly a hundred thousand dollars? And you didn't know it was there? No wonder the FBI and everyone else was so interested. Still, as she'd been saying, cash is not a crime.

"The next rumor is that we are suspending our day-to-day ministries because of lack of funds. That is true. And the next is that we're being sued. That is true as well."

Nearly the whole congregation gasped. Gracie realized that she had, also.

"That is, we are not being sued directly. We're involved, however. A man named Harold Mayhew insists that the sum discovered in the church here is his life savings, stolen from him recently. He is suing for possession.

"The final rumor pertains to —"

But Gracie didn't hear. She was still trying to figure out this Harold Mayhew business. How would his life savings disappear and then reappear in the church? He was not a member. Why had the police

71

blotter, which Rocky published periodically in the *Mason County Gazette*, not mentioned the theft, if theft it was?

Then Barb again motioned *rise* for the congregational hymn. She whispered, "Change: 322. Hear me? Three two two."

Three twenty-two. Gracie snatched up the hymnal and leafed feverishly. Here it was. She smiled. *I'd rather have Jesus than silver or gold.* So true.

Harold Mayhew. How perplexing. All that money. Just as perplexing!

Pastor Paul led the closing prayer. The congregation filed out into the rain as the choir sang to them. Rain or not, it's a nice way to leave a church. This was a piece the choir frequently had some trouble with. Tish Ball and Tyne Anderson, the Turner twins, tended to lose both the pitch and the tempo and thereby throw everyone else off. Today, however, Estelle's attention-getting soprano, normally an intrusion, saved the day by drowning the twins out.

The service had ended. The choir folded their sheet music and silently stole away. No, not silently, exactly. The old wooden stairs would not permit "silently."

"I think we should go talk to Harold Mayhew tomorrow," Marge murmured to Gracie as they hung their robes up.

"It's not our business," Gracie reminded her. "And it's a legal matter, Marge. We could do more harm than good."

"You're dying to learn more, same as I am. I know it!"

"Yes, but if there's a lawsuit, we could do damage."

"Not if we keep it casual enough."

"And just how casual is 'casual enough'?"

"My business license needs renewing in a month or two. I'll just drop by the town office tomorrow and do it a little early. Coming along?"

How could Gracie resist?

Against her better judgment, therefore, she found herself with Marge at the Willow Bend municipal building early the next morning.

Normally, Marge complained whenever she had to deal with her town's rules and regulations. Today, however, she took the bureaucratic setbacks not just with good grace but with eager good grace.

Said the clerk with a frown, "This isn't due until February next year."

A colleague chimed in, "Why would you want to renew early? You have plenty of time."

As they were waiting for the reluctantly

completed paperwork, they watched for the custodian named Harold. They peeked into rooms and glanced around corners.

Finally, the clerk banged her rubber stamp on the last bit of paper. "There you are. The display copy will be mailed to you in about two weeks."

Marge had her renewed business license, but they had seen neither hide nor hair of Mr. Mayhew. They walked out into the empty hall.

"What a bust," Marge sighed. "We've been through the whole building."

"Not quite." Gracie headed for the exit stairs. "Back when El was in office, Harold was something of a slacker. He's probably not any less a slacker now. We've been looking in all the wrong places. We've been searching up here, where he would be working."

"Where would he be not working?"

"Let's try the furnace room." Gracie led the way to the basement.

They threaded among overhead pipes and conduits slung so low that even short Gracie had to duck occasionally.

She called, "Harold?"

"What?" A clunk accompanied the response.

Gracie entered a windowless room

through a rickety old door whose green paint had nearly all peeled off.

Illumination in this recess consisted of one naked light bulb hanging overhead. A huge coal furnace filled half the room. By the door, a table served as a desk. None of the dust-covered papers scattered across it seemed to have been touched in years. An ancient metal kitchen chair sat near it. This whole place felt depressing to Gracie, extraordinarily so.

In the corner beside the furnace, Harold Mayhew sat in a dark brown wooden captain's chair. Gracie realized what the clunk had been; this skinny, withered little fellow had just brought the chair back down to all four legs.

He sat scowling at them. "What do you want?"

Now what? Gracie and Marge could hardly say they were lost or that they had come here by mistake. Who would proceed this far without knowing they were in the wrong place?

Marge smiled broadly. "Why, I believe you *are* Mr. Mayhew! Am I right? Are you Harold Mayhew?"

"Yeah. Why?" He eyed them suspiciously.

"Mr. Mayhew, you are a legend in your

own time! A wealthy man who prefers a simple life working at the job he loves. Has Mr. Gravino talked to you yet?"

"The newspaper editor? Why would he want to talk to me?"

"Why, because you're famous, and you live right here in Willow Bend. If that's not the perfect subject for a Sunday feature story in the *Mason County Gazette*, I don't know what is."

"Me? Famous?"

"Of course! You're —"

"In the paper?" He scowled again. "I don't think so."

"But think what a model and inspiration you would be to young people!" Marge declared. "You are teaching them by example that money isn't everything. Young people are so greedy, you know. They need your lesson."

"I'm the only one supposed to be down here. Maybe you oughta just —"

"And your attitude toward safeguarding your wealth is so unusual! I can't imagine simply misplacing nearly a hundred thousand dollars."

"Misplacing? That money was stolen from me!"

Gracie shook her head. "But Harold, you never reported it as a theft, did you?"

"Who'd believe an old man? They'd just say I was making it up to get attention. But I will have what's mine, you hear? Now, both of you get out."

Marge dug through her purse for a business card and a pen. "Gracie? What's Rocky's number again?"

Gracie recited his work number.

Marge jotted it down and ventured close enough to Harold to lay her card on his knee. "Here's Mr. Gravino's phone number. I'm sure you'll be hearing from him soon, but if you don't, do call him. Ta ta!" She waved cheerfully as she disappeared back into the hallway.

"Good-bye!" Gracie followed Marge out the door.

They retraced their steps from the musty gloom into the bright, open halls upstairs. They continued outside onto the steps.

The sun had not emerged yet, but at least the rain had stopped. Gracie basked in the light and drew in huge breaths of wonderful fresh air. In just the few short moments she was in it, that basement had driven her nearly to distraction.

And she didn't doubt that Harold Mayhew had already been driven to the very same place.

10

Uncle Miltie came out of his room with his shoulder bag slung loosely across his back. In essence a backpack with one long carrying strap instead of short ones, it enabled him, with his hands occupied by the walker, to carry things more easily.

"Are you going shopping?" Gracie was curious.

"Maybe. Maybe not." Uncle Miltie hastily headed for the front door.

Now what's going on? Sometimes he frets or seems put out with me, but this feels more like furtiveness.

But what was on her own to-do list? Going over to the municipal building in search of Harold Mayhew this morning had gouged a big dent in her day. She still had not done the week's household shopping; neither had she picked up the dry cleaning that had been ready last Friday. And half a dozen bills and letters lay on her desk clamoring for attention. Ah well. She could do all that in one afternoon.

A few brief hours ago, Marge had taken Rocky's name in vain, so to speak — and certainly without his knowledge. Had it occurred to her that she should mention the matter to Rocky? Probably not. Gracie added to her list, *Stop by paper.*

When she eased Fannie Mae out onto the street, Uncle Miltie was nowhere to be seen. She stopped at the dry cleaner on the way to the newspaper and carefully laid the plastic bags in her trunk. One item done.

If she was going to answer the correspondence on her desk, she'd need stamps. She added *post office* to the bottom of the list and scratched out *dry cleaning.* At this rate, she was not gaining any ground.

Lists. What a blessing and a nuisance they were.

As she pulled into the newspaper's parking lot, she noticed a huge black van with the vanity plate TOOTLE. Who on a newspaper would put "tootle" on the license plate? She went inside.

She stopped by Judith's desk. Rocky only thought he was the boss; Judith Depopoulos was the one who actually ran the paper. She always knew where everyone was, what they were supposed to do, what they wanted (sometimes when they themselves did not have an inkling), and how to

79

get things done. Rocky merely acted as editor and publisher.

"Is Rocky available?" Grace asked.

"No and yes." Judith inclined her head toward Rocky's cubicle. "His ear is being bent against its will by the high school band director. You go sit in that leather chair closest to his desk. When he says hello, indicate that you have an important private matter to discuss. He desperately needs a reason to give Phil Murphy the old heave-ho."

"I don't want to intrude."

"Oh, yes, you do! It will be your good deed for the day."

Still a little reluctant, Gracie wove between desks to Rocky's hideaway. She paused by the entrance.

Rocky saw her and grinned. "There you are! Sit down, Gracie. I'll be right with you."

As per Judith's orders, she perched in the leather chair beside the desk.

With his tone of voice, the other man sitting there made it very obvious he considered her an unwelcome intruder. "We're, ah, not quite finished here."

"But almost." Rocky dragged his keyboard into his lap. "Okay, Phil. Give me what you know — facts and figures — and

I'll look into it. You know Gracie Parks, don't you?"

"Chief Bower has all that. I gave the police a complete report . . . Yes. Hi, Gracie."

Rocky sat back and laced his fingers behind his head. "Fine. But you said you wanted me to investigate. Do you want me to work with whatever little tidbits Herb decides to toss me, or do you want me to work with all the facts?"

"Why would he withhold anything?"

"Why should he bother giving me any info at all? He's not obligated."

"Mm." The band director glanced disapprovingly toward Gracie. She attempted to look innocently unaware of the distraction factor she'd introduced.

Rocky asked, "You want me to publish this in the paper for everyone to read, but you don't want this woman to hear anything?"

"She belongs to Eternal Hope, I know. That's all."

Gracie was not accustomed to being referred to in the third person. It felt funny.

Rocky poised his fingers above his keyboard. "All right?"

"Very well. Here's the company's promotional material." The band director set some brochures on Rocky's desk. "You see right there how much money they promise.

81

They say, if we install and service their soft-drink machines in at least three locations, we'll make this much right here. We've got four, but we don't. We're just not making what they say we will."

"Mm hm." Rocky clicked rapidly on his keyboard. The stereotypical newspaperman types with two fingers. Rocky used at least nine. "And where are the coin-op machines located?"

"That shouldn't make any difference. They said —"

"Where?"

The band director sighed. "One on the high school campus, one at Celebration Lutheran, one at Bethesda Methodist and one at Eternal Hope. The high school machine and two of the church ones do fine. It's only the one in the activity room of the Eternal Hope Church that isn't turning a profit."

"Who has keys to that church's soft-drink machine?"

"Paul Meyer — he's the pastor there — and their senior warden. Also Jimmy Briggs, of course. He's the student in charge of our fund-raising. Jimmy services all the machines. Jimmy and Eddie. Eddie's his best friend. Both are in the brass section. Good players."

Rocky asked Grace, "Is Jimmy Briggs a

member of your church?"

"No," she replied. "I believe his parents go to Celebration Lutheran."

Rocky clicked some more. "So if Jimmy services the church machine, Phil, why do those people need keys?"

"In case their machine breaks down. These aren't new machines. They're re-conditioned. It would have cost more to install the newest machines."

"Well," Rocky said, "if Chief Bower is apprised of this, I would think he'd investigate the matter pretty thoroughly and —"

"He doesn't think a soft-drink machine could make that much — you know, as much money as they found. So he's not paying much attention to me. But those machines certainly can turn that kind of profit. This is how the marching band gets the money to travel."

"Amazing," Rocky commented. "But you still haven't proved anything."

"Look at it this way," Phil Murphy added. "Whoever took it, a church would be the perfect place to stash the stolen money, right? That's what it is, you know. Stolen."

"Yes. I see." Rocky nodded gravely. "Since churches offer sanctuary to people, you think it's logical that they offer it to money, as well."

11

Gracie watched Phil Murphy depart through the crowded newsroom. "I would think," she mused aloud, "that someone who directs a marching band would have a little better co-ordination than that." He'd just bumped into a desk, knocking off a stack of books.

"And more common sense." Rocky sniffed. "It's logical that the church's soft-drink dispenser isn't going to be making as much money as the others. Your activity room is open how often?"

Gracie saw what he was saying. "The youth group meets Friday nights. It's booked for other things now and then, and a Good Samaritan breakfast once a month. That's what? Eight or nine occasions a month, for a few hours each?"

"Right. So it's not used much. While the one at the high school is right out in front of the kids, handy, all day long. When I brought that up, he brushed it off. I'm sure Herb Bower mentioned it too." Rocky put his keyboard aside. "Thanks for helping cut that session short. I owe you. Now what can I do for you, fine lady?"

Gracie pondered, perplexed. "I've forgotten! When the band director started talking about how Eternal Hope is swimming in cash, I got distracted. Where would he get that fool notion?"

"Not so fool. When you've got a cool hundred grand salted away in your loft —"

"I thought it was a bit less than ninety grand."

"Well, sure. I was rounding off." But Rocky's facial expression, and his tone of voice, told Gracie instantly that he had let something slip. But what? And was it something big?

"Aha! I get it!" She nodded. "The official figure being released is ninety, but the actual amount was a hundred. And the police are hoping that the owners, whoever they are, will start bickering, one of them thinking another has stolen some of it. Or is holding some back. And if that seed of distrust grows, they could make a mistake; you know, do something to attract notice and get caught."

Rocky stared at her. "I can see that I should never underestimate you. But, then, I never do."

"Good!" Gracie thought about all this a

moment. "Of course, the thief accused by the other thief or thieves could simply say that the twister carried away the missing part."

"True. May I buy you some coffee?"

"Sure." Gracie stood up.

Rocky ushered her out the door, as they decided on Abe Wasserman's delicatessen. On the way over, Gracie remembered to explain to her friend what Marge had done to his good name.

Since their friend Abe was out, they got their coffee "to go" and took it down the street to the old Carousel Pavillion, at the edge of Fairweather Park.

The pavillion did not currently have a carousel. It had had one once, however, back in the twenties, and the city fathers vowed it would have one again. But carousels, even the cheapest ones, were extraordinarily expensive, so the plan was not an immediate-priority item. Gracie and Rocky, therefore, sat on one of the benches arranged on the huge circular pad in lieu of a merry-go-round. Even under the gray sky, sitting out in the open there felt quite pleasant.

Gracie sat silent awhile, thinking. *If the object of the soft-drink vending machines was to raise funds, why did they put one in the*

Eternal Hope back room? It was a very nice convenience for the few people who either worked or served there frequently, like Pat Allen (who always brought her thermos), or the youth group and others who used the facilities sporadically. In fact, Gracie had assumed that the vending machine belonged to the church, or at least that its profits weren't going to a third party.

"So Marge took my name in vain," Rocky chuckled. "Doesn't matter. My name's suspect anyway."

"Oh? What's the matter with it? And should I be seen sitting with you?"

"It's the other way around. I shouldn't be seen sitting with you. Gracie, remember that these law enforcement officials are all very, very suspicious of everybody else. To an FBI or other agent, nobody is innocent. So here we have a pretty hefty chunk of change stashed in a closet. That's suspicious. No ifs, ands or buts. So what if the closet is in a church? That just means one or all the church members are suspect. It's in the choir loft. So the choir members are the prime suspects. Following me?"

"They suspect *me?!*"

"Bingo." Rocky sipped a moment. "But then, Lester Twomley invited me in to give them a guesstimate on repair costs, since we had that little problem with the roof on our own building last year."

"Also, you report every bid in the paper, so you know what the current climate is. You've seen them all."

"Right. Astute of Lester, really. I'm a good one to ask. So I gave him and Delano my thoughts on it. Now. The enforcement folk ask themselves, 'Why would a newspaper editor, of all people, be brought in to submit an estimate on something like that? Completely out of his field. Hmm. Very suspicious. Let's see how much they pay him for his services.' So now I'm tied into it."

"This just gets crazier and crazier." Gracie grinned inwardly. Rocky was so adamantly nonreligious, and yet here he was, cast into the same pot as those suspicious church folk. Ironic, to say the least.

Rocky finished his coffee and stood up. "The next thing they'll be doing is looking for under-the-table payments made by the church to me. Ostensibly for consultation, but really to keep my mouth shut about a clandestine operation in the church involving big bucks. Or, possibly, in payment to me for my involvement in it. My cut." He raised an eyebrow at her, then winked.

"Oh, now that I hear that, I have to say

crazy is putting it mildly. I would never in a million years be able to think up something so twisted, let alone suspect someone of it."

"Trust me. Those clowns think of nothing but."

They walked in silence out to the street and back toward his office. Together, they dropped their empty paper cups into the trash receptacle on the corner.

Gracie mused, "I wonder who's following us just now, if anyone."

Grinning, Rocky shrugged. "Let's just hope they don't bump into each other. With so many interested parties, and no one claiming the money whose story our visitors believe, it's getting pretty crowded in Willow Bend."

"But it's not a case, Rocky. No wrongdoing has been found yet, or even hinted at. All there is is money."

"Money is enough, Gracie. Money is enough."

12

"This way, please, ma'am." The uniformed young woman ushered Gracie into a small room. There were several rows of chairs in front of a large mirror. Gracie had never been in this part of her local police station before.

"Have a seat there, please. It's very nice of you, Ms. Parks, to come on such short notice. We called you and you responded immediately. We appreciate that."

Gracie really, really wanted to say, *My day was shot anyway. After talking to Rocky and learning about all those suspicions, I've been dismayed and confused. What in the world will anyone think of next?* Instead, she said, "My pleasure." Ah, the burden of being polite!

The young woman was not a Willow Bend officer, Gracie felt sure. Her name tag said, simply, Desmond. No help at all.

Her voice sounded as though she was re- citing from a prepared script. "From the choir loft, you choir members can see nearly all the pews — that is, almost everyone who attends services. Now, we are going to bring out several groups of people. Each person will step forward in turn and rotate so you can see all four sides. You are to tell me if you think that person has ever attended a service at Eternal Hope Church, even once. Also, if you recognize anyone in the line-ups by name, please tell me. They're behind glass. They can't hear you."

Behind glass? So far, Gracie saw nothing but the chairs in this room. The lights in the room dimmed. Then the huge mirrored window revealed its purpose: Six young men filed out, obviously being directed by a voice to their left. The first one glanced offstage and stepped forward. He turned a bit, turned again, again, again.

Gracie shook her head. "I don't recognize him from any angle."

The next did likewise.

"Oh. That's Chuckie Moon. Charles Moon. He used to have an earring. I see he got rid of it. And he dyes his hair various colors. I rather like the off-blond shade he's chosen now."

"He attends your church, then."

"No. I don't know that he worships anywhere. He used to be interested in Angela

Billingsly, but that's over now."

The young woman studied her. "You know all this about him, but he doesn't go to your church."

"You're not from a small town. I can tell."

The next young man stepped forward. He was unfamiliar to Gracie. Of that whole batch, Chuckie was the only one Gracie had seen before.

Whoever set this up salted the next batch of six — this time women — with two girls from the late service.

"We have an early and late service on Sunday mornings," Gracie explained. "No music at the first one. The choir sings at the second. And hardly anyone who attends the one regularly ever goes to the other one. It's almost as if there were two churches. So there may be people coming through here who attend faithfully but I never see them."

The next batch contained Hannah Cates. Gracie explained what she knew of Hannah, though it was precious little. The woman still had her wary look about her and kept glancing off to the side.

The new group included Lester Twomley. Gracie dutifully identified him. She also recognized the young man who worked for Anderson's Meats and Hammie Miller, who operated the grain elevator and feed store.

They filed offstage.

"This next will be the last," the young woman promised.

The designation for this final line-up had to be Little Old Men. Gracie felt like giggling. Suddenly, she clapped her hand over her mouth and burst out laughing. These were certainly no Napoleons of crime!

For here came Uncle Miltie clumping onstage in his walker! He looked exceedingly disgruntled, his mustache bristling visibly.

The first old fellow stepped forward. "He's a friend of my uncle," Gracie said. "They play pinochle together." That second man once drove the school bus and now helps out Roy Bell. "And Ben McIver there is married to Eleanor, a friend of mine."

It was Uncle Miltie's turn. Glaring at the offstage director, he clumped forward two steps. He didn't bother moving the walker. He simply turned around inside it and clumped back to the line.

"This is a joke, right?" Gracie said.

"Hardly! This is a serious matter, Ms. Parks, and we expect your full cooperation."

"Pushing my eighty-year-old uncle out into a line-up where he obviously doesn't want to be is not cooperation, Officer. Yes, he attends Eternal Hope regularly, and I can give you his complete history. How many hours of it do you want to hear?"

Said Ms. Desmond huffily, "We did not realize he was your uncle. We're sorry if this has caused you any inconvenience."

"Oh, it doesn't cause me any inconvenience, but he doesn't exactly look ready to break out into song . . . or any illegal activity, either."

The young woman said only, "Thank you very much for your cooperation, Ms. Parks. You may go now."

Gracie sat. "Not quite yet, if you please." She twisted around to face her squarely. "I could not see any pattern in the line-ups, as you call them. And I realize that there does not necessarily have to be one. However. You included a choir member, Lester Twomley, in one of the groups. If this actually were a matter of choir members identifying people in the pews below, as you said, he would not be there. He would be here with us."

Sounding flustered, the young woman repeated, "You may go now."

Obviously, Gracie would receive no answers here. She nodded to the woman and left.

She knew where she could find answers, perhaps. Lucille Murphy, the police dispatcher, might be able to help.

Gracie crossed the nearly deserted squad room and peeked into a side office. Lucille sat there at her work station, manicuring her nails. The screen-saver on her computer monitor flicked from a picture of Bryce Canyon in oranges and golds to a scene on the Oregon coast in grays and blues.

Gracie stepped inside. "I was going to ask if you were busy, but I guess I won't."

Lucille laughed. "It's been awfully slow the last few days. I almost like it better when it is busy. Like, right after the twister. Wasn't that something? Sit down, Gracie. How's that goofy cat of yours?"

"Gooseberry is just fine, thank you. I'm sure he'd send his love, if he ever thought about it."

"I'm sure! He's a neat old cat. Tell him I said so."

"I shall." Gracie perched on the edge of the chair beside Lucille's station. "Do you know who that young woman is over in the room where they do line-ups?"

"Stuffy young trick with short brown

hair? Roberta Desmond, from Chicago. Cold as an Eskimo's lawnmower and sharp as a baby bottle. She's here working for ATF, but she seems more like a rent-a-cop hired for the occasion. They brought her in yesterday. She's pretty green."

"Who does she work for?" Gracie still was unclear which law enforcement bureaucracy she'd been dealing with this time.

"Alcohol, Tobacco and Firearms," Lucille explained. "Pretty soon we'll have everyone here but the Coast Guard."

"What are they doing, lining up all those people?"

"Haven't a clue. You know in *Casablanca* where they round up 'the usual suspects'? Well, those were ours. Vagrants, a couple underemployed folks, plus some ordinary citizens they borrowed for the occasion. They were very hush-hush about it."

Unfortunately, that didn't tell Gracie anything. She tried to think of some reason that made sense.

Lucille leaned forward, saying in a conspiratorial whisper, "I don't know which man is the one or which woman is the one, exactly. But I know for sure that one of those women is a stranger to town called Hannah Cates and that one of the men may be her husband."

13

"Oops! One of the boys has got himself a speeder!"

Lucille shifted her attention instantly from Gracie and the manicure to a scratchy radio transmission that was coming in at that moment.

Gracie tried to make out what the radio voice was saying. But she could not even tell for certain which officer it was, let alone discern any words.

Lucille obviously had no trouble. She responded. The garbled voice recited a number. Lucille typed it into her computer as he spoke.

She swirled her mouse around on its pad, clicking here and there, and then sat back. "Everybody else's police force has computers right in the squad car. The officers can trace registration and stuff themselves. Not here. Willow Bend is still in the previous century, computerwise."

Gracie stood up. "I should try to salvage something from the day. It was good to talk to you, Lucille."

Lucille grinned and waved as she dragged her keyboard in her lap. "Go ahead, Car Two."

Gracie wandered out the door, wondering why she had been summoned here, really. And why ATF would be interested in anything to do with Eternal Hope. Or what she was going to feed Uncle Miltie and herself for dinner.

She got halfway across the squad room, headed for the exit, when a mountain of fury charged in. She froze.

Chief Herb Bower could intimidate her under the mildest of circumstances. Now the palpable anger he exuded frightened her, even though she knew perfectly well how silly her fear was.

He paused and glared at her. "The ATF suspects foreign thugs. Seen anyone foreign-looking lately, Gracie?"

"Herb, what in heaven's name is going on?" She hoped he was angry enough to let her in on some of what was really going on.

"I'm losing my own jurisdiction, that's what's going on! Foreign thugs, for crying out loud!"

"Herb?" Lucille called from her lair. "Grzbovsky on three!"

He snatched a phone off the nearest desk and slammed the receiver to his ear. "What?" As he listened, he rolled his eyes to the ceiling. "No, we don't have any 'Most Wanted' poster people in the area, and if we did, I'd probably send my kid out to collar them and collect the reward." He listened a bit. "You better believe I'm being facetious. I'm getting pretty fed up with you guys." He listened again. "No, I have no idea why Mrs. Grace Parks would be summoned to the station here, but I'll be happy to ask her for you. It'll save you bothering her." He grunted. "Believe me, sir, it is no inconvenience. Hey, Gracie? Why are you here? She says she'll tell me later." He listened briefly, said good-bye and hung up.

Gracie crossed her arms. "Actually, Herb, I was hoping you could tell me why I'd been asked to come by."

He settled down just a bit. "So you really were summoned. I thought you just dropped in. Come on into my office." And he led the way.

He waved her toward an oversized chair. Gracie perched herself on it and found it so comfortable that she slid back immediately and nestled in. She described her most recent adventure to him, careful not to omit details. She asked him the question she had asked Ms. Desmond: Why was Lester in the lineup? And he couldn't answer it either.

He shook his head. "I don't even know what she thinks they were doing. They just sort of moved in.

"Gracie, I sure wish your El were still here. He was the best mayor we ever had. He stepped back and let us do our job, and if something like this came up, he'd run interference for us. The Feds would never have muscled in the way they did now."

"But why did they?"

"I wish I knew. It can't be *just* the money in your church attic. I mean, ninety thousand isn't —"

"A hundred."

He smirked. "Who told you?"

She smiled sweetly.

"Okay, let's say a hundred. That's peanuts these days if you're talking about drug or gun trafficking. You can hardly even buy an informant for that anymore. And another thing. Grzbovsky heard you were called in, but he didn't seem to know it was ATF that did it. They're tripping all over each other. It's hardly a model of interagency cooperation."

Gracie nodded. "You're saying that it's

more like a rivalry. That they're each working independently."

"Yeah. Are they all that bored in these regional offices, that they have to come out to the sticks and bedevil ordinary citizens?"

"I hope that's a rhetorical question. All this is certainly extremely confusing. There's nothing logical about it, unless we're missing something major. And since so many of them have descended upon us, I would guess that we're missing *something*."

"I run a good department, Gracie."

"As good as any bigger force," she agreed. "Most important of all, we — that is, private citizens — can expect fair enforcement, and you can't hope for any better than that."

"Thank you. I think so, too." He pursed his lips a moment in thought. "But, except for us Bowers, none of my people goes to Eternal Hope Church."

"I'm sure that doesn't automatically consign them to hell, Herb."

He laughed out loud. "Well, I can't ask Marybeth — she's at home with the kids. But you're around there all the time. Gracie, how would you like to be a spy for me?"

"Spy on my own church?!"

"Not a spy, exactly. An informant. I need the inside skinny on what these feds are looking into and looking for. I'd like to know if they're hassling Paul Meyer and if so, what about. Stuff like that. I want to know why they're here, and I'm sure not going to get a straight answer out of them."

"But I'm quite certain I'm a suspect, at least in their eyes."

"So am I, probably. Look." He waved toward his wife's photo on his desk. "The money showed up in the loft. You sing in the loft. But so does my wife. So I could be involved, too. Seriously, you're a natural for this. Plus, I know *you're* not guilty, and you know *I'm* not guilty."

"Oh dear. Let me think about this." *What I really mean, Herb, is, let me pray about this. Any quick hints as to what I should do, God? Or should I apply more time in prayer? Show me a sign, please.*

And then a thought dropped into her head so instantly and so clearly that she had no doubt it was divinely inspired.

She said, "I assume you trust me."

"Completely."

"So do my fellow church members, and I will not betray that trust. I would love to help you get to the bottom of this, but not by going behind Paul Meyer's back. I will not discuss our little spy project here with any church member, or even with the secretary. But I will help you only if I can confide my job, so to speak, to Paul. Him alone. But him."

"Now he *is* a suspect in my book. But yeah. If you'll feel better about this by doing that, do it."

He said yes to my request. Good sign, God!

And thereby, just that quickly and easily, occasional amateur sleuth Gracie Parks became (drum roll): Gracie Lynn Parks, Master Spy.

14

It was raining hard as the newly minted espionage agent drove home from the police station. Gracie mused ruefully that Herb could not have chosen a more appropriate informant. She and Marge were now scheduled to go over to the church in the morning to do the filing and other office chores that had been postponed. She would be privy to everything happening in the office. And though she already had Pastor Paul's ear, she'd really soften him up if she took in a home-baked apple pie.

Impulsively, she turned her car in the direction of Eternal Hope. If she swung around by the church and picked up Pat's diskette containing the church bulletin, she could make the appropriate changes at home and thereby cut their time at the office there considerably tomorrow.

She approached Eternal Hope from the "good" side — the side without the ugly gash in its roof. She slowed. A woman was hovering among the trees beyond the church's back parking lot. What was Pat doing out there?

It wasn't Pat. Gracie pulled into the church lot but did not park out front in her usual place. She drove on around to the back. With a mighty turn of the wheel, she swung Fannie Mae wide and pointed her nose toward the trees.

The woman had stepped back farther among the trees, so far that she was probably up against the trim little rail fence that marked the property line. Gracie saw now that she had a child with her. There they went, the two of them, jogging away along the fence. The child was small enough to have a hard time keeping up.

Gracie cut the motor and leaped out. "Wait!"

The woman did not pause, but when she crossed a clear spot, Gracie got a pretty good look at her.

Hannah Cates.

Gracie was getting very wet. She flopped back behind the wheel and closed the door. What in heaven's name was Hannah doing back here?

Gracie did not try to pursue her. Hannah obviously did not want to be seen, and there were half a dozen ways she could have gone once she reached the end of the property. Gracie eased her car back around to the main parking lot and slipped into a slot near the door. This rain was so heavy, and neither poor Hannah nor her child had been wearing a raincoat.

She snapped her door open, leaped out, and slammed it behind her as she lunged from dry car to dry porch.

At her desk in the secretary's office, Pat Allen peered over stacks of papers nearly as high as she. "I thought you were coming in the morning."

"I can do some of the next bulletin at home, if I can take a diskette."

"Gracie, you're wonderful. Now if I could just find the diskette box." She scowled at the jumbled ruin of her desk. "Those insane investigators. They delivered a court order this morning to see all our books and supporting receipts for the last four years. Four years! A lot of the things they think we should produce don't even exist. And our treasury was a train wreck anyway. I'm not a violent woman, Gracie, but I could throttle that Bill Smyth! Imagine, claiming to be a Wharton grad. Ex-con's more like it."

Gracie pondered this a few moments. "Did we ever do a background check on him?"

Pat stared at the wall a moment. "No. We needed an instant replacement because Becky had to cut way back on her commitments after that mini-stroke, and up he popped. When a person offers to do a job like that, you don't think —" She winced. "You don't think. Period. That's the whole point, isn't it?" She returned to her rummaging.

"Pat, what was Hannah Cates doing out back?"

Pat stopped to stare at her. "She was here? Behind the church? I have no idea. She didn't come in. Maybe she's another one we should do a background check on. She didn't look like she was trying to break in or anything, did she?"

"No. Just standing there with a child, as if waiting for someone."

"Weird. Ah! Here's the disk box." From beneath a hopeless-looking pile of papers, Pat dragged a plastic box designed to hold fifty floppies. She pushed aside a large full-color folder of roofing samples to make room, although it was not that big a box. She rapidly fingered through it and found a red diskette. "Here you are. Thank you in advance, Gracie. It's one less job I have to fret about."

Gracie made small talk a moment or two

and left. On impulse, she walked to the back of the church and peeked out the window in the back classroom. Neither Hannah nor the child was anywhere around.

She then made a mad dash back to her car and leaped in. As she drove home, she realized she was still full of questions that had no answers.

Putting Fannie Mae in the garage, she stopped to spend a few minutes simply watching the downpour through her back door. *Rain really is a lovely gift, Lord. An essential one. When people complain about it, I'm sure it's because they don't realize how important Your gift is.*

Thank you!

Opening the refrigerator, she studied the collection of leftovers. There weren't many. Oh, wait! Away in the back, hidden by the sourdough starter, was that cooked chicken breast left over from the breast of chicken Florentine she'd made Sunday. There was more than enough for green chicken enchiladas. Perfect! She had onion. It was already chopped, in fact. She had a small can of mild green chilis. She also had some frozen anaheim chilis, but she'd save them for relleno sometime.

Uncle Miltie slipped into the kitchen behind her. "What are you making?"

"Green chicken enchiladas. Dinner around six?"

"Gonna be leftovers?"

"Almost surely. There's plenty here."

"Good. They make a good lunch, you know." And he purposefully made his way toward the door.

Gracie turned to look at him. "You're properly dressed for the weather, but. . . ."

He offered from beneath his hooded yellow rain slicker, "I noticed something going on out there, yeah."

Considering his mood, she obviously didn't dare suggest he stay home. "Your walker's going to rust!"

He ignored her and started off.

She sighed. He was an adult. She was not his mother. At times, those two facts intruded too plainly on what she wished she could say or do.

She sautéd the chopped green chilis and the onion as she cut into small pieces the cooked chicken. She was combining everything with garlic and a can of cream of celery soup when the phone rang.

She tucked it against her ear with her shoulder as she stirred. "Hello?"

It was Marge. "I'm still at the shop. Are we set for tomorrow morning at the church office?"

"Yes. I'll drive, if that's all right. How'd the job interview go?"

"What a dope! He had all the people skills of a grizzly bear with a hangnail." The voice hesitated. "Is something wrong?"

"I don't know. Uncle Miltie is acting strangely."

"And your point is . . . ?"

"I mean, stranger than usual. He seems furtive. Perhaps agitated. We don't seem to have the easy closeness anymore."

"Gracie, that's normal! He just watched a tornado whiz past him. People act strange for a while when they've just escaped a disaster."

"I suppose."

Marge's voice was reassuring. "He's a resilient old cuss, Gracie. He's seen trauma before. Let him work it out. He'll do fine. Maybe that mustache he's grown is affecting his brain!"

Gracie laughed. Still, she was concerned.

I'm sure Marge is right, Lord. But I appeal to You anyway. Please lift him up. He hasn't gotten that police lineup squared away in his mind, either, I can tell. But it's something more than that, I feel sure.

He must never find out that I laughed, back at the police station, that is.

15

"Uncle Miltie? We're going now," Gracie called from the back doorway. Did he hear her? She walked into the dining room and repeated, "We're going now."

"I heard you." Uncle Miltie came stomping out of the bedroom. "Good-bye. Don't get lost."

His prickly attitude was still puzzling her. She added, "We intend to be back by lunch."

"Don't know if I'll be around then or not."

Apparently this was the end of the conversation. Gracie said good-bye and went back out through the kitchen. "Gooseberry? You didn't eat breakfast."

With the supreme disdain only a cat can express, he stared at Gracie, his eyelids at halfmast.

Marge showed up as Gracie left the house. Her hair was drawn up and back this morning. She usually wore it thus when she was prepared to work. She hopped into the passenger side of Fannie Mae and looked at Gracie. "*Now* what's wrong?"

"I don't know. Gooseberry and Uncle Miltie are both behaving strangely. I understand about the post-stress thing, but Gooseberry wasn't near the tornado. Why is he acting peculiar?"

"When does he not act peculiar?"

Marge had her there.

When they arrived at the church, Gracie was unable to park in her usual slot. It was taken by a media van. She had come to dislike such vehicles immensely. Emblazoned with the station's logo and burdened with that big dish on the roof, it occupied more than its fair share of the church's front entryway. Its doors hung open.

"We're still a news item?" Marge frowned at the intrusion.

"Apparently." Gracie followed Marge through the doors and back to the office.

Marge stopped in the office doorway and bent backward to look up and down the hall. "Where's Pat?"

"I'll look upstairs. You try the food bank closet."

Gracie jogged halfway up the back stairs to the choir loft and stopped cold. What was going on up there? She slowly, quietly, completed the climb.

Brilliant lights illuminated the torn-apart cubbyhole, that infamous once-and-always stash. One of the perfectly coiffed women Gracie had seen on Uncle Miltie's morning news program was speaking into a microphone as her cameraman dutifully filmed away. Looking indignant, she was waving an arm toward the hole in the roof as she spoke. Well behind the camera, Pat stood disapprovingly with her arms folded tightly across her chest — for, beside the reporter, Harold Mayhew was gravely nodding.

The reporter extended her mike in front of the old janitor's mouth. "And your money would probably never have been found if it weren't for that freak of nature. Is that what you're saying, Mr. Mayhew?"

"I'm an old man," Harold said. "This church is supposed to be caring about people, and here's my life's savings stolen! Yeah, it'd be gone forever and theirs to keep if it hadn't got blown out all over Willow Bend. I'm just grateful that twister went through when it did, or I'd be destitute, know what I mean?"

"And can you prove it's yours? You have to —"

"Shouldn't have to prove it. It's mine!

Nobody else can say that. Not and be truthful, they can't. Let 'em prove it's not mine."

Pat saw Gracie and came over to the stairs. She looked miserable.

The reporter wound up her segment, but Gracie didn't hear it exactly because Pat was mumbling something *sotto voce* about opportunism. They went back downstairs together, Pat leading the way into her office.

Gracie paused in the doorway. "What is going on up there?"

"I got blindsided." Pat explained. "They said they wanted to do a brief segment. I said, 'Fine.' The next thing I know, someone's leading Harold Mayhew through the door. They trooped right up the stairs, and there they were. They didn't mention a thing about Mayhew when they got permission."

Gracie thought about this a moment. "On the other hand, our policy is to never turn anyone away."

"There's nothing in the church bylaws about news teams." Pat picked up a stack of manila folders. "These need filing. And the library catalogue is about three months behind. Charles brought in all those old books, and they're not entered yet." There were also many old issues of *Guideposts*.

To work, to work.

They completed the filing in a little over an hour. The books, boxed and waiting to be shelved, were stacked in the back room.

Marge pulled down the first carton and popped open the flaps. "Oh, my. Look at some of these!" Then she glanced out the window. "There she is again."

"Who?" But Gracie knew whom.

"Hannah, of course. You told me about seeing her there yesterday. There she is. Isn't that about where she was when it was raining?"

"Yes. Under the same tree, even. And there's the little boy with her." Gracie asked, "So what do we do? She ran the last time I tried to speak to her."

Marge sniffed. "Bet I know why she's needing charity. The twister blew away all her money."

"But I thought it was being claimed by Harold Mayhew."

"Isn't that ridiculous?"

From the doorway, Pat spoke. "Maybe not. I was just talking to the cameraman. Harold might be able to make such a good case in the media that public opinion will sway things his way, know what I mean?"

Marge frowned as she scooped up handfuls of books. "The way I understood it, if the cash doesn't belong to anyone else, we get it."

"That was mostly Fred," Pat added. "He says we should simply say that an eccentric benefactor left it to us that way. His intent would be that someone would be digging around in a closet sometime and bingo. There it is."

"That's pretty silly, too."

"Fred says not. He started brainstorming, and he decided that if we didn't find it in a certain time, then the benefactor could simply begin to send hints to go look somewhere. Anonymously. He came up with all that at the lunch meeting yesterday."

Staring off into space, Marge speculated, "I wonder how many other people like Harold Mayhew are going to come popping out of the woodwork before all's said and done."

"Greed." Gracie scooped up an armload of uncatalogued books. "It's so sad. Everyone is so eager and waiting to grab money." She glanced out the window.

Hannah Cates and the child still stood by the tree.

They were quite obviously waiting.

16

"I think a general appeal for funds is the way to go. Bake sales and rummage sales don't get you enough money fast enough." Pastor Paul looked from face to face at his assembled church board. At the far end of the conference table, Estelle recorded feverishly, her brow wrinkled and the tip of her tongue caught between her teeth.

Halfway down the conference table, Gracie sat confused. This morning when she and Marge helped Pat, they had seen Hannah Cates lurking, and yet they had ended up doing nothing. It was not, Gracie hoped, a lack of compassion. It was the uncertainty of not knowing what to do. *Lord, why did Hannah run away when I tried to make contact in the rain that time? I could have helped her. Now, at this emergency board meeting, I don't know what to do again. Why do I feel that I most wish to do nothing at all? What a horrible frame of mind, so unChristlike! And I do want to be like Your Son. Please give us direction. Please help.*

But, at least as far as Gracie was concerned, no help appeared to be forthcoming.

"Gracie," Paul said, "you know Rocky Gravino well."

"We're friends, yes."

"I'm thinking we could place a half-page ad in the paper, maybe a full-page ad, letting the community know we're cash-strapped, with no insurance, and need to look for assistance in paying for our repairs."

"Why should nonmembers care enough about us to give us money?" was Fred's entirely logical question.

"Eternal Hope is a community landmark, Fred. This is one of the oldest buildings in town and we maintain it well. Except for the minor problem of a big hole in the roof, it's well kept up. We're an asset to Willow Bend."

"What do you want me to do?" Gracie asked.

"Two things. One is to put together an attractive ad to run in the *Gazette*. The other is to see what kind of deal you can cut with the paper to publish it. Since this isn't a public service announcement, it would most probably be considered a regular ad. But these are special circumstances. What do you think?"

The request slightly irritated Gracie, and at first she couldn't imagine why. She finally figured out that it felt like he was trying to take financial advantage of her friendship with Rocky. But it was her church's future that was at stake, and she understood that the minister was simply focused on his goal, mustering his resources as best he could.

They spent the next two hours discussing why or why not an ad was a good fund-raising idea. Gracie listened not just to hear the various arguments pro and con but to pick up ideas. What would be the best way to formulate the ad for the *Mason County Gazette*?

Eventually, Pastor Paul's suggestion came to a vote. The vote passed by show of hands.

Gracie waited until the meeting closed to approach the pastor. "I can't do this ad alone. I'm just not sure what to say that will encourage contributions best."

"I'll be glad to help you, Gracie," he assured her.

Gracie drove home that night feeling absolutely muddled. But then, why not? The quiet life of at least one simple choir member was shattered. This was her church, so long a close and dear part of her life. What if its very existence depended now upon her skill in creating an appealing advertisement for it?

Early the next morning, she headed off to the editorial office of the *Gazette*. If she were really fortunate, Rocky would not be particularly busy this morning. Surely he would help them. After all, he was an experienced hand at writing copy.

She waited a few minutes at the convenience store across the street. Pastor Paul rarely arrived anywhere on the dot, and today he was his usual few minutes late.

"Good morning." Gracie greeted Judith as she walked in with Paul. "Is Rocky available? We have a problem he will be able to help with."

"He's working on the layout of Sunday's edition."

"Well, do you think we could just have a few minutes of his time?" Gracie ventured. "I hate to impose. . . ."

"Sure. He'll kick you out if he's feeling under the gun." She made a face to indicate mock-fear.

Indicating they understood, Gracie and Paul crossed over to the editor's office, entering with apologies. Rocky seemed willing to hear them out, so Paul explained the church's crisis and the proposal for running an advertisement in the *Gazette*. Gracie hoped she was concealing well any of the discomfort she felt and wished Paul could be a little more eloquent. The problem was, he was worn out and distracted by all the tough situations he was supposed to be managing.

Rocky sat back in his chair. "You've got a right to take any ad you like in my paper. And I know Gracie's here with you, Meyer, because of her loyalty to the church to which she has belonged for nearly all of her life. I also know that the other night I suggested you go directly to the public with a plea for funds to help out."

"But, now, what I think is that you've got to explain to me, to my complete satisfaction, just what that stash of cash in your choir loft is all about. Convince me that it could have been there without your knowledge and that there's a perfectly innocent reason why a church that collects offerings every Sunday in its sanctuary is concealing bundles of dough that don't seem earmarked for good works."

Paul was silent. So was Gracie, who was willing him to speak up and make Rocky see the righteousness of their request and the sincerity of their need. It wasn't just for their sakes she cared so much — she knew Rocky's often antagonistic manner hid a softer self — but for the sake of the families to whom Eternal Hope meant so much.

Rocky grunted, indicating he was waiting for the young man sitting in front of him to say something, anything.

To Gracie's horror, however, Paul Meyer, her pastor, made no answer.

17

The morning news blared from the kitchen table. Someone up on the corner kept blowing a horn as if to urge someone else to hurry up. The garbage collection truck, a little behind schedule today, groaned and screeched out back. Gooseberry curved against Gracie's ankle as she entered the kitchen. He meowed loudly.

Her day was beginning in cacophony — not a good portent with choir practice scheduled that evening.

She greeted Uncle Miltie as she got a can of cat food out of the cupboard.

And froze in her tracks.

She had just heard the phrase "Eternal Hope Church" emanating from the television!

"Hey! Come listen!" Uncle Miltie waved at her.

The news reporter she'd seen interviewing Harold Mayhew now stood in front of the ripped-apart section of the church's choir loft. She was wearing the same neatly tailored suit and looked just as blandly officious. She gestured toward the hole — but she wasn't talking about the money.

The screen next offered a talking-head shot of Herb Bower, who was saying that half a dozen people had already filed claims, each insisting that the money the twister had revealed was theirs.

Then the screen returned to Harold and the reporter as Gracie had seen them. At the time, she had not picked up on the tone of that interview, having heard only a portion of it. Now, though, she grudgingly allowed that the young woman reporter was a lot sharper than she had first given her credit for.

Skillfully, the reporter was drawing from Harold exactly what she wanted him to say. He believed he was simply sounding off in order to get his life savings returned to him, playing upon public sympathy. But the truth of the matter was, he was playing right into the reporter's hands, illustrating splendidly the theme of this brief news segment.

As she wound up the bit with her capsule summary, the young woman reiterated the theme.

Greed.

"I doubt that this is going to please Harold." Gracie returned to the matter of cat food, for Gooseberry was pestering her in earnest now.

Uncle Miltie commented, "Herb doesn't look too mightily pleased either. Dyspeptic, you might say."

Gracie brought the can to the table. "I know he doesn't like all the media coverage we're getting. And he's absolutely working on a coronary trying to deal with the assorted law enforcement agents scampering around the countryside. I don't think I've ever seen him quite so angry and impatient."

She popped the can open and fed Gooseberry. She refilled his water dish. Then she prepared herself a big bowl of bran cereal with sliced bananas. She cleaned up some milk Uncle Miltie had spilled before it dried on the countertop. Finally, she was able to sit down and dip her spoon in her bowl.

On the table, Uncle Miltie tapped the newspaper with his finger. "Did you see this?" What he was indicating was Rocky Gravino's editorial, a piece that with a great deal of innuendo and several levels of sarcasm questioned the propriety of a church with obviously suspicious funds stashed away looking to amass more.

It depressed Gracie to read it, especially because it caught her up between two loyalties. She knew her friend Rocky was wrong to suspect her Pastor Paul of major malfeasance, or even of ever robbing a cookie jar. But she also knew she as yet had no way to convince him of his mistake. Where *had* that money come from?

On one level, the mystery of its origins was none of her business, nor was the ultimate dispensation of the funds any of her concern. But it was her church that was involved, and so the puzzle intrigued her even more than it might have ordinarily. There simply had to be a logical solution, and she hungered to find it.

"Uncle Miltie, do you have anything for the dry cleaner?" She would, at least, take some action, she decided.

"Only my dry humor."

"Hmm." Gracie was thinking.

After breakfast she gathered up her silk blouse and linen suit. She would drop them off at the cleaner, and, as it happened, the dry cleaner was quite near the newspaper office. She could just happen to stop by and tell Rocky personally what she thought of his editorial.

But as she drove downtown, wisdom got

the better of anger. What specifically would she achieve by barking at the editor? Nothing. How best could she counter his stubborn insistence on coming to the wrong conclusion?

She wouldn't yell at him. Instead, she would write a letter to the editor, pointing out what she believed had to be the truth, that Paul was merely in a state of shock, not hiding anything. Since he himself had no idea where the money had come from, he was simply too honest to throw out creatively plausible explanations.

Somehow, in today's world, the one saying "I don't know" was always the least believable.

Sighing, she composed the letter in her head as she parked at the dry cleaner and awaited her turn in line. She almost wished — no, she *did* wish — she could wake up and find out the tornado and its aftermath would all turn out to have been a dream.

But it wasn't. And Gracie soothed herself by remembering one of the longtime favorite sayings in her household: "God keeps life mysterious but that doesn't mean you should stop trying to figure it out."

18

That evening Gracie, who normally regarded the kitchen as an area of creative pleasure whether she was catering a party or preparing a family meal, was all cooked out. She adored fixing food when she was in the mood, but there were moments when she was as far away from that mood as a body can get. This was one of those times. On the bright side, she had been cooking enough these last few nights that there really ought to be a full-course meal of leftovers tucked away in the refrigerator.

This, in fact, would be an excellent "Musgo Night," as in, everything in the refrigerator "mus' go."

Only Gooseberry was getting fresh grub. She would serve him cat food, as usual.

Gracie was expected at choir practice in a bit over an hour, and Uncle Miltie was not yet home. Where in the world was that man disappearing to these days? He was ever and always a wanderer, but never before had he absented himself this much.

She opened the refrigerator and put on her thinking cap. Perhaps the chicken potpie from two days ago would serve as a good entree. She poked around among the shelves. Curious. It was gone. Uncle Miltie must have heated it up for himself for lunch. But why hadn't he mentioned it? He usually did.

How about the broccoli-and-noodle casserole? If she added in some canned salmon, there would be enough left for two. But she couldn't find that, either. And the little container of leftover pot roast and gravy was missing, too.

She closed the refrigerator door, the better to think about it a moment. The containers themselves were gone. She didn't remember seeing them in the sink. She swung open the dishwasher door. They weren't there. Did he wash them out and put them away? But, no, the containers weren't returned to the plastic-container bin.

She was going to have to cook, after all, and she was going to have to do it quickly. She didn't have much time left before choir practice.

She opened the cupboard door, studied her array of canned goods, and called on the Muse of Quick Cooking to strike.

The Muse came through. There sat a can of chopped clams. Butter? She had just purchased a pound Friday. There should be plenty. She opened the fridge again and found a single stick. A can of clams and a stick of butter would have to make a meal for two.

She got out a package of angel-hair pasta and set the water on the stove to boil it. As she waited for it, she chopped two onions and brought in the mail. Gooseberry followed her out and back. He curled against her shin as she stood at the stove.

As she melted the butter, she wondered about this whole new puzzle. She knew her kitchen well. Something had changed and, whatever it was, things weren't quite right. She began to search.

There should be at least four cans of fruit cocktail in the cupboard, because she'd recently bought six on super-special. She found one. The package of shell macaroni was still there, unopened. So were the cans of tomato sauce and about the right number of cans of stewed tomatoes. But the peaches were gone, as were most of the soups. Canned water chestnuts and bamboo shoots? Here. The canned chicken and tuna? Not.

Gooseberry by now had settled himself

at the very middle of the kitchen floor. He curled into a C, stuck a hind leg straight up, and began a careful bath.

Would Uncle Miltie even be back for dinner? He had left no word. That was uncharacteristic of him. She put a two-serving portion of angel-hair into the bubbling water, considered a moment, and emptied in the rest of the package as well. She would cook it all and freeze the leftover, or serve it later with some other sauce. She stirred the chopped onion into the melted butter. While the onion slowly turned translucent, she dumped in the clams, liquid and all. Salt, a generous dollop of minced garlic and several heaping tablespoons of parsley completed the sauce. At least none of the herbs or spices looked to be missing.

Neither were the salad vegetables in the crisper. She brought out the whole drawer and started ripping lettuce. She would toss a salad for herself. She would wait until Uncle Miltie came home to make him one, so that the lettuce would be fresh. You don't freeze leftover salad.

Now there was a thought. Was anything missing in the freezer? She looked, but she found that she couldn't remember precisely what she had put in there. She saw no big empty holes in the motley collection of ice cream, meats and packages of vegetables.

The angel-hair cooked *al dente*. No Uncle Miltie.

The angel-hair cooked to almost soft. No Uncle Miltie.

She needed to leave for the church in half an hour.

She turned off the heat and drained the pasta. If Uncle Miltie came in now, he could reheat his dinner in the microwave.

She dressed her salad, got out the grated Parmesan cheese, spooned the butter clam sauce over an ample serving of angel-hair and sat down to eat.

Bored with his own toilette, Gooseberry had wandered off.

Gracie Lynn Parks, who had decided not to cook tonight, had in fact whipped up quite a nice meal. She wished Uncle Miltie were here to enjoy it with her. But mostly, she simply thought. She pondered. She mused. She considered.

She completed her dinner and put the dishes in the dishwasher. She combed her hair and got her purse. As she walked out the door and drove Fannie Mae to the church, her thinking had produced an idea and a possible solution, plus a sneaky plan to test that solution.

She could not yet solve the riddle of the mysterious appearance of money in the loft. She could not yet say why so many law enforcement officials assumed that discovery of the cache lay somehow within their purview. But she had a pretty good idea where all her leftovers were going.

She would enlist Marge's services in this. In fact, she might require the help of the whole choir. *Now Lord, You know me as no one else does. You know my innermost heart, so You know I am not normally a sneak-around type of person. But if we are to get to the bottom of this, You and I, I'm going to have to become absolutely devious. I thank You in advance for the help You are about to provide. Amen.*

19

The night before, after choir practice, not a single cloud had shown in the sky. Totally clear. Now, look. Cold rain pattered on Gracie's poncho hood and threatened any moment to go down her boots.

She folded her arms and drew them in close to her chest. She should have worn an additional sweater.

"This is nuts," Marge grumbled. "He's not going to go roaming in weather like this." She shifted from foot to foot beside Gracie.

"Rain doesn't seem to stop him. I even teased him his walker was going to rust!"

"I had to leave practice early last night, before you finished setting up your spy team. Who else is taking turns following your dear uncle?" Marge's hair, so carefully coiffed before she left her house this morning, now drooped in weary semi-ringlets around her ears. Her little rain hat was cute but didn't do much to keep the persistent rain at bay.

"Don has off this afternoon, so he can help if necessary, and Amy is going to take over when school lets out. Lester says he'll do a turn tonight if Uncle Miltie goes out after dark. But he rarely does."

They stood hidden behind the ancient privet hedge at the end of the street. *Thank You, Lord, for the positive response from my fellow choir members. That was Your work, I'm sure.*

Marge switched feet yet again. "This is almost as much fun as a root canal. You did turn off your cell phone, didn't you?"

"Yes, but thanks for asking. It would spoil everything if I got a call while we were following him. He'd hear it for sure."

"And you really think Uncle Miltie is your thief."

"Of the leftovers, yes. He's the only one with easy access. And you'd have to have easy access to make off with so much."

"And what if it's just your own aging brain playing tricks? You know, forgetting what you have and don't have."

Gracie made a face at her friend. "Come on, Marge! Let's say a twenty-year-old forgets something. You dismiss it as being thoughtlessness, or preoccupation, or just a lapse. When an older person does exactly the same thing, you say, 'Oh, her mind is

135

slipping! Old age! Pity.' When it's not old age at all! It's the same occasional lapses she's had her whole life!"

"I know, I know," Marge replied soothingly. "Don't practice ageism. But give me a break! My lapses aren't occasional anymore, and neither are yours."

What Gracie would have come back with, she didn't know, but it didn't matter: show time. "There he is!" she suddenly whispered.

Leaning forward to balance the pack on his back, Uncle Miltie came down their sidewalk to the street, not with his walker but with his quad canes.

Gracie stepped back farther behind the hedge. Marge pressed in close beside her. Gracie's poncho crackled when Marge bumped into it; Marge quickly stepped away.

Hidden, they listened as their quarry came bumping up the street in this direction, his canes making soft noises as they struck the pavement. He passed them and continued to the corner. The little bumps paused and varied as he let himself down one curb and up the next, then grew too faint to hear.

Cautiously, Gracie peeked out around the hedge.

The rucksack on Uncle Miltie's back sagged with weight. He occasionally bought something that would be that bulgy and heavy, and he would bravely tote his purchase home. But almost never did he carry something heavy away from the house. Instead, he would ask Gracie to deliver it in Fannie Mae. And most of all, he would not be out in the rain on some errand unless there was some overriding importance to doing it at once and secretly.

The women silently fell in behind him, following, and Gracie felt a certain satisfaction at having her suspicions confirmed. They gave Uncle Miltie at least half a block and often more. Why risk being detected? He was surely not going to disappear anywhere in a hurry. He plodded stolidly along, his canes thumping out at either side of him as he pole-walked down the street.

They reached an alley. Gracie carefully peeked around the phone pole at the corner. She felt a little like the nattily attired young woman on the covers of all those Nancy Drew mysteries, always undetected and never in the rain. Except, she was in her sweatpants.

Her uncle had covered almost half a block. He stopped and turned to look this way. Gracie ducked back and waited. Had he seen her? She peeked again.

The house on the far corner of the alley, clear out on the next street, had been standing vacant for at least six months that Gracie knew of. Uncle Miltie seemed to be headed for that house's garage. The garage faced onto the alley.

"Uh, Gracie?" Marge whispered.

"Wait. He's still there. He'll see us if we move now."

"Uh, Gracie!"

"Ssh! He hasn't lost much hearing."

Marge tapped her on the shoulder.

Impatient, Gracie turned. "What do you —" and froze.

It wasn't Marge.

Grinning like the Cheshire cat, the humorless FBI agent, Martin Grzbovsky, said, "Ms. Parks. You're being detained for questioning. Come this way, please."

20

"Very well," Gracie said, "I will explain it for you one more time, beginning to end."

Agent Grzbovsky sat across the little table from her and stared at her, his arms firmly folded. On the table in front of him lay a legal pad and pen, but though he didn't seem inclined to make any notes. They were in a room of the Willow Bend police station.

"Among all the other puzzles around here lately, my uncle, George Morgan — he's Uncle Miltie to everyone — has been acting strangely." Gracie paused, then continued. "That's not at all like him. He's bottling something up. My cat has been acting secretive also."

"Your cat. You didn't mention the cat before." Was that a note of sarcasm she detected in Grzbovsky's voice?

"Gooseberry. He's — well, he's a cat. You know, very catlike — but still, lately he's been unusually reserved or cautious, like Uncle Miltie. Anyway, I noticed yesterday that not only have all our leftovers disappeared, so have the containers."

"You count leftovers?" The man's voice stayed flat.

"I don't have to. They're gone. Logically, only Uncle Miltie or I would have ready access to the fridge, and I didn't take them. Therefore, he did."

"I see."

"Also, canned goods are missing. The thief takes foods that are easy to prepare or need no preparation. Foods that are ingredients of more elaborate dishes aren't touched. So it's really a pattern, do you see what I mean?"

"Keep going."

"So last night at choir practice, I organized a group of us to keep an eye on him. You know, find out where he's going and what he's up to. He had to be doing something with that food. This morning when he left the house, Marge and I followed him to that alley. Unfortunately, thanks to you, we don't know where he was going from there."

"Why would any of the other choir members care?"

"They don't, personally. But they're my friends. I'd do the same for any of them."

"When did you first notice food was missing?"

"As I said, late yesterday afternoon. Once I did, I started hunting for it in earnest, and checking out everything else at the same time seemed logical."

"And the other choir members are such good friends that they jumped right in to help solve the mystery, is what you're saying." He looked skeptical. "When did you last see the woman who calls herself Hannah Cates?" He looked pleased with himself.

The question caught her off guard. He had not mentioned her before. "A couple of days ago."

He stiffened and his expression changed slightly. Her answer obviously had caught him off guard. Tit for tat. "When exactly?"

"I don't remember exactly. It was the morning after you let our secretary, Pat, return to her office. I still, by the way, can't imagine that all that was really necessary."

"Under what circumstance did you meet her?" He ignored her last comment.

"I didn't meet her. You asked if I saw her. I did, but she wasn't in hailing distance."

Liar! All you had to do, Gracie Lynn, was

open the rear window of the church and call to her. And you didn't.

Gracie beat her conscience back into submission. But it wouldn't stay there. It kept prodding at her. *You have seen her more than once, and you haven't even been trying to help her since that first day.*

"Very well, where exactly did you see her?"

"Behind the church."

"What was she doing there?"

"Waiting. Standing there. I don't know."

"Did she have a man with her?"

"No. A boy, maybe ten."

"Describe him."

"Thin. Dirty-blond hair. Nothing about him especially stood out." Gracie had detected hostility in this man, and it had seemed directed toward her. He acted as if he didn't believe a word she said. And yet, his hostility, perhaps even anger, now seemed focused even more on Hannah than on her.

"Describe Jason Cates."

"Is that the other boy? She mentioned having two."

"The husband."

"I've never met the husband."

"Then how do you know he exists?"

"I don't. In fact, our church secretary

says that she's known welfare applicants to invent them."

"Ms. Parks, why are you lying to protect Hannah Cates?"

And there, Gracie's mind churned to a stop. How in the world does one answer a question like that?

Grzbovsky pressed on. "Why were you loitering in that alleyway? Whom did you expect to meet there? Hannah? Or perhaps the husband?"

"Loitering?!" If her brain had screeched to a halt a moment ago, it was grinding into reverse now, or possibly galloping away out of control. Loitering! Of all the silly, nonsensical conclusions to draw. "Mr. Grzbovsky, if this is typical of FBI detection, I'm surprised you people catch anyone at all. I was *not* loitering, and I was not waiting for anyone. I've told you several times what we were doing."

He sighed, then irritatedly said, "We know the truth, Ms. Parks. You might as well come clean."

"The truth?"

"Your partner in crime, Marge Lawrence, confessed everything. Don't you think it's time to tell us all about it?"

Gracie felt like the runaway stagecoach in the old B westerns she had seen as a child. Always, the hero at great personal peril would ride up to it and climb aboard as women and children screamed inside it. The hero would fall, catch himself somehow and eventually gather in the reins to stop the wild-eyed horses. The whole scene was utter nonsense and could never have unfolded as they filmed it. No matter. It implanted itself in her memory anyway. And just now, her brain was acting like that runaway stagecoach.

She drew a deep breath and began gathering in the reins.

"Ms. Parks, I asked you a question."

"I am thinking." But that was not exactly true. What she was doing was attempting to get her horses under control.

"Mr. Grzbovsky. Item number one. You cannot expect to obtain the truth by lying. There is no way Marge would confess, so to speak, to untruth. And besides, item two, you've been with me, and she has been with that other gentleman, since we arrived here. You have no way of knowing what they're talking about, let alone be apprised of some confession. I suggest that you do not lie to me again."

"Ms. Parks. . . ."

"And another thing. I spent the best years of my life married to the man who made them the best. I prefer the honorific Mrs. because I earned it. You will address me as Mrs. Parks, please."

"Mrs. Parks. . . ."

Gracie raised her voice. "You are obviously certain that we were lurking for some clandestine reason. I suppose that since we're members of Eternal Hope Church, it all is somehow connected to the hoard of cash you can't make any sense of. I point out that you have no reason to make that assumption. I also point out that to the best of my knowledge, there are no ordinances in this town against loitering. We've never needed them before, nor do we now."

"Mrs. Parks. . . ." He was beginning to look a bit frustrated.

"And I further point out, Mr. Grzbovsky, something that all you federal employees keep forgetting. There is no law against cash!"

"Mrs. Parks. . . ." This time, Mr. Grzbovsky was interrupted by a knock at the door. Scowling, he got up and opened it.

Either Herb Bower or Rocky Gravino could practically fill a doorway simply by standing in it. How full the opening looked with the two of them standing there! The cavalry had arrived.

Mr. Grzbovsky snapped at them, "I'm not done here yet, gentlemen. I can talk to you later."

Herb raised a hand and stepped inside. "We thought we'd drop by and just listen in. It's no trouble for us, really. Don't worry."

Rocky entered too, looking confident and flashing a reassuring grin at Gracie.

Agent Grzbovsky fumed, "This is not a press conference! I'm conducting an investigation and I will not have it compromised."

Herb answered carefully. "You might consider me a small-town cop, but I know reasonable cause and a few other precepts you're ignoring. The thing is, we small-town cops don't take well to folks coming in and trampling on our citizens' rights and protections. Understood? This interview is ended."

Grzbovsky made a decent effort of trying to stare Herb down. Gracie could have told him it wouldn't work, but decided simply to sit back and watch. Suddenly the agent broke his gaze, snatched up his unused pad and pen, and stormed out.

Grinning, Rocky stood up.

Herb made a sweeping gesture toward

the door. "Mrs. Parks? You're free to go."

"Thank you, Herb." Gracie stood up, in no hurry. As she stepped out into the squad room, she saw the two FBI agents leaving through the far doors.

"The one thing worse than criminals breaking the law is law officers ignoring it. Gracie? Rocky? I need your help. And Marge Lawrence's and everyone else's. We've got to find out what's going on here."

21

Lunch time. Well, almost.

Gracie, Herb, Rocky and Marge stood in the middle of the squad room, no one making the first move. Gracie looked at Marge and Marge looked at Gracie. She gave a slight nod.

"Our FBI friends are gone for now and it's lunchtime," Gracie said sweetly. "May we treat you two gentlemen to lunch?"

Herb glanced toward Rocky. "What do you think? Suppose we should be seen eating with criminals?"

"Why not?" Rocky nodded to Gracie. "Where?"

But, in the end, no one saw them because they decided to order in sandwiches from Abe's Deli. Two roast beefs on rye, one turkey club and a small tuna sub.

While they waited for the food to arrive, Gracie asked Marge, "Did they think you knew anything about Hannah Cates?" Marge nodded. "Well, me, too," Gracie went on. "Guys, what can you tell us?"

The two men looked at one another. Herb spoke first. "We think that the Cateses are professional rest area bums. You know, they have a big cardboard sign, hand-lettered, saying they need money because of car trouble and they're Christians, so please help."

"They trot out the whole family, too, kids included," Rocky added. They had obviously pooled their information.

"This Hannah has a sort of a record. She's been picked up for loitering in Morgantown, which is how Morgantown takes care of homeless people. She was arrested for petty theft in Gary, but the charges were dropped. Other than that, nothing on the computer to help us on her."

"Agent Grzbovsky says the husband's name is Jason."

Rocky nodded. "And the sons are Tim and Bradley. Tim's going on eleven and Brad will be eight, if he lives long enough."

"What does that mean?"

"Well, I have a source at the hospital who checked for me to see if there'd been anyone named Cates needing medical attention. I was just curious and it paid off. . . ."

Just then Lucille Murphy, the daytime dispatcher, buzzed Herb to let him know that their lunch had arrived.

Rocky continued. "Hannah and her youngest boy turned up there a week or ten days ago. Severe asthma complicated by diarrhea. Myself, I saw a lot of kids with stomach stuff like that when I was in the Peace Corps. But that was in Bolivia, among poor farming families in remote villages. What can you expect, when the Cateses don't have a home? And then the mom seemed convinced he was going to die any day."

"That's terrible!" Gracie almost shouted, then quickly lowered her voice. "Do you think it's really true that the poor woman has no hope her child can survive?"

"Yeah. I believe it, even if I don't have much to say for the way she provides for her family."

Marge shook her head sadly.

"We picked the husband up on a complaint from the mini-mart manager," Herb added. "But we didn't hold him. He didn't really do anything, just looked bedraggled."

"Then why arrest him?"

"The store owner votes for councilmen, to whom I answer. Cates doesn't. He went in the back door of the police station and then out the front just that quick."

"Your turn again." Gracie turned to Rocky. "What were you doing at the police station? Why do you and Herb suddenly seem to be in cahoots?"

Rocky didn't answer her for a moment, pausing to take a large bite of roast beef and a swallow of coffee. And when he did, it wasn't directly. "When there's a chance to slay a dragon and rescue a damsel in distress, I know I, for one, will always take it. Er . . . two damsels," he amended, glancing at Marge.

"Well, you should have seen Agent Grzbovsky's face when I told him I had enlisted other choir members to help follow Uncle Miltie, and —"

"You what?!" Herb interrupted, nearly choking on his food.

"He's *my* uncle and I'll follow him if I want to. Anyway, it's a long story."

"It had better be a good one. We're already up to our ears in trouble, all of us."

Rocky snorted. "Maybe we can get adjoining cells so we can play pinochle." But he didn't seem much worried about either crime or punishment as he savored his last bites of the oversized sandwich.

After all, for the moment, anyway, they were already the guests of the chief of police.

22

Gracie nibbled at her share of the special slices of poundcake Abe had included in the lunch delivery. She had just finished explaining to the men about the missing food and her attempt to follow Uncle Miltie.

Herb's only comment had been, "That agent may not be the only one around here who's paranoid. Missing leftovers, for Pete's sake!"

Now as Marge and Herb bantered, Gracie thought about all the depressing things that were currently going on in Willow Bend.

The conversation paused.

"Rocky," she said, "I'm still mad at you about that editorial. It just wasn't like you."

"It's what I believe."

"I know. That's what irritates me most."

"I told you. I just don't like it that the church is looking for charity at the same time it's got some mysterious involvement with a very unexplained bundle of money.

A *big* bundle of money."

"Okay," Gracie replied. "That's your opinion. You're utterly and completely wrong, but I'll wait to say I told you so."

"*We* don't have anything to do with the money or the FBI or even Hannah Cates. Not really," Marge added. "Even if we do belong to Eternal Hope."

"But they knew you were following Uncle Miltie." Rocky now looked less serious, more amused.

Marge's eyes went wide. "They were following us? The FBI was following *us?*"

Gracie casually waved a hand. "Oh, they've been doing that ever since they got here. But I thought they'd given it up."

"Of all the nerve!" Marge was incredulous. She complained to Gracie, "Anyway, they ruined our shot at finding out where your uncle's going. We got all wet for nothing. But, actually, I'm getting kind of curious myself. What do you think he's really up to?"

Gracie looked thoughtful. "I have my suspicions." She suddenly grinned. "But what I'm *really* wondering is how long that money was up there before it drifted out of the sky to give us so much grief. That's what we've *got* to find out."

23

"Gracie?" Amy Cantrell's voice on the phone sounded concerned.

"What's wrong, child?" Gracie held her kitchen phone with her shoulder as she stirred the evening's entree, her personal casserole invention, Chickahominy Succotash.

"I can't find my wallet. Did I have it at practice last night, do you remember?"

"Oh, my. Let me think." Gracie stopped stirring. "Yes. Yes, I think you did. Didn't you get your wallet out of your purse to make change for Lester for the Coke machine?"

"Yes! So maybe it's still there, do you think?"

"Quite possibly. Do you have a key to the church?"

"No."

Gracie thought about this a moment. "When do you need it?"

"At seven tomorrow morning. I'm going on a field trip and I'll need my student

I.D. and lunch money."

Gracie added the seasoning. "Dinner will be ready here in half an hour or so. I can go over to the church afterwards and bring it down to you — assuming it's there, of course. Would you like me to do that?"

"I didn't mean to make you have to go to that much trouble."

"I wouldn't suggest it if I wasn't happy to do it for you. If it's not there, nothing's lost. At least, you'll *know* it's not there."

"Thanks, Gracie!"

"My pleasure, Amy. Blessings."

As she turned her full attention back to the succotash, she thought about the many threads from around the world that wove the fabric of her daily life. Take this one-pot meal right here.

It was her mother's recipe, based not upon any family tradition or old cookbook but upon an engraving of a painting by an artist, John White, done around the year 1590 in Virginia. Mr. White recorded for-ever the lost civilization of the Powhatan confederacy. In one work, "They're Sitting at Meate," he showed a man and woman seated at a common bowl. Gracie's mother had devised the recipe from what the In-dians pictured seemed to be eating — a dish of hominy, beans, fish and corn. Of course, Gracie's mother being Gracie's mother, she'd added a few extra ingredients, such as garlic, celery and onion. She had left out the clams shown in the engraving, while Gracie herself sometimes included chopped bacon or ham bits. The resulting savory dish was a favorite of Uncle Miltie's regardless of what went into it, and it had always been one of Gracie's as well.

Uncle Miltie arrived home ten minutes before Gracie was ready to dish it out. While he washed up, she made the salads and set the table for two. In the middle of the table, she put out the succotash casserole. She poured the appetizer — tomato juice — into glasses and set one on each plate, along with fancy napkins. She put the Tabasco bottle next to his place. Her uncle liked to spice up his "cocktail," while Gracie preferred hers straight.

The table quite nicely appointed, thank you, she sat down.

Uncle Miltie couldn't help exclaiming, "Mmm! Good," as he eyed the succotash appreciatively. He invoked the blessing then, with perhaps a bit more gusto than when the entree was, say, liver and onions.

Gracie sipped her tomato juice. "I had a

very informative conversation at lunch today with Herb and Rocky."

Uncle Miltie shook the Tabasco well and jolted out three large dollops. "What'd you learn?" He stirred and sipped.

"That the federal agents consider us all suspects, whether we like it or not."

"Suspected of what?"

"That's what puzzles me. As far as I know, no crime has been committed. It just isn't stopping them from trying to find one." Presently, she asked, "What do you know about Bolivia?"

He looked at her oddly. "Now why'd you ask that?"

"Just curious. Rocky mentioned being there in the Peace Corps."

Uncle Miltie's facial expression said, *There's a reason you asked that you're not admitting.* His voice said, "Mostly farmers, about half, I think. Half Indians. Two capital cities, La Paz and Sucre, and they do different governmental things in each. Wide range of climates, from the Andes above treeline to low tropical forests — Amazon stuff — and farming in between. It's a big source of cocaine and heroin, probably because somewhere in Bolivia you can find a climate that's perfect for anything you want to grow."

"You know more about it than I expected."

"Took geography in high school." And he tackled his succotash with determination.

Gracie had taken geography also. She knew better than to believe that was his source. Obviously, he had boned up on Bolivia lately. But why?

Every time she tried to solve even the slightest little puzzle, she not only failed, but a bigger one popped up. Gracie would let Uncle Miltie open the next topic of conversation.

They finished the meal in silence.

She took her dish to the sink. "I have an errand to run for Amy Cantrell. I'll be back in an hour or less. I believe it's your turn to tidy up the kitchen."

He mumbled something and stood up. No *Good-bye*. No *drive safely*. No *Where are you going?* And yet, his curiosity was normally as sharply honed as hers.

She picked up her purse and left.

She was nearly to the church when the illogic of his lame response struck her. Back when he and she took geography in school, the production of cocaine and heroin was not an issue.

She parked Fannie Mae at the front door

and let herself in. She climbed the stairs to the choir loft, each step creaking as she put her weight on it. As she switched on the light, she looked over at Amy's chair. She walked behind and pushed it a little out of the way, the better to examine the floor around it.

No wallet. Poor child. Losing all your cards and I.D. was a vexation anytime, but if she needed it tomorrow morning . . . wait! Over there!

The wallet lay against the balustrade, nearly invisible in the shadows. Gracie reached for it and froze. Crouched against the wall, it gaped open; its coin purse flap was not snapped. This wallet had been rifled. And Amy could not have dropped it here. She sat over there and would have exited in the other direction.

Carefully, Gracie grasped it by two fingers and stood up. There might be fingerprints on it, she reasoned, and they might answer a question or two about who had been prowling around up here.

She could not imagine a choir member stealing anything from one of their own, or even thinking of doing so. This had to be the work of an outsider. And yet, why Amy's wallet? And how had anyone had access to it *in* the choir loft?

Perhaps Amy had put down or dropped her wallet at choir practice and inadvertently left the church without it. Then the prowler, the person who'd stashed the money in this loft, came up here and saw it, removed whatever was of value, and tossed it aside.

Still handling it by the edges, Gracie checked to make sure. Yes, it was Amy's. The picture on her student I.D. was a very nice likeness. But the money pockets were empty.

Still holding the wallet carefully, Gracie turned out the loft light. Raw blackness swarmed around her. She gave her eyes a few moments to adjust, realizing as she stepped away from it that she should have walked over to switch on the stairway light before she extinguished the room light.

She stopped, and listened. A stair creaked, and then another. Someone was coming up!

Her eyes had adjusted sufficiently that she could just see a very vague outline, black on black, before her.

In the dark stairwell she stood face to face with the intruder.

24

Prayer raced through Gracie's head faster than she could think it.

"Who is it? Who's there?" she called out.

The apparition backed down a step. Its voice sounded just as terrified. "Who are you?"

"Gracie Parks."

"Gracie?" The voice hesitated.

God finally fought His way through the thick wall of her terror and reached her with His gentle hands. She realized, then, that He was in charge here, regardless of how it might appear. Curiously, that did not much reduce her fear. But it made it manageable.

She firmed her voice. "You're Jason Cates, aren't you." No response. She kept talking. "I can't see your face, but the outline doesn't look like anyone I know at church here. At least in outline, you don't look like any of those federal agents, either. So Hannah's husband is the next best guess."

"Agents?" He moaned, "Oh, God!" but it did not seem to be a blasphemy. It sounded more a plea for help from a panicky, distraught man. He repeated it. Then, softly, "Oh, Hannah!"

Gracie had no idea what to say next, if anything. She wanted to get around him, to reach for the light switch that he obviously did not want on. Unmoving, he blocked the stairwell.

He stammered a moment, then stated despairingly, "My little boy is dying." He turned, clattered and stumbled down the stairs, nearly falling, and sped toward the back of the church. Throwing on the light, Gracie rushed down to the soft, welcome pad of the hall carpet. She ran outside, unsure now in which direction the young man had fled.

Leaping into Fannie Mae, she jammed her key into the ignition, and sped out of the parking lot.

Herb Bower's home, she knew, lay a scant four blocks away. Gracie drove there, screeching to a halt at Herb's front curb, and ran for his porch.

Herb burst out the front door. "Who do you darn kids think you're —" He stopped. "Gracie?"

"I just saw Jason Cates —"

"But he's not a fugitive or any—"

"— in the church."

"I'll be darned!" Herb rushed back inside. Grace followed just as quickly and closed his front door behind her.

Beyond the living room archway, he scooped a radio transmitter off the buffet. "Gladys! Get Jimmy over to Eternal Hope Church. I'm on my way." He dipped his head. "Come on, Gracie."

In bedroom slippers, jeans and his white T-shirt, Herb led the way out his kitchen door. His chief's patrol car sat in the driveway. As Gracie followed him, Marybeth Bower leaned her head out of the upstairs front window. Startled to see Gracie, she grasped immediately that there was no time for explanations. Waving, she disappeared back into the house.

Somewhat out of breath, Gracie ran to the passenger side. The door lock clicked and she slid onto the seat. She slammed the door and groped for the seatbelt.

"Okay." Herb backed out of his drive. "Why is a lady of a certain age screeching her brakes in front of my house like any teenager?"

Gracie laughed in spite of herself and told him what had happened as they roared with lights and siren awhirr the four short blocks to the church.

As Herb turned the corner into the church driveway, Gracie saw Jimmy drove in from the other direction. Dousing the lights and siren, Herb continued on around to the back of the church and parked in silence near that rear window.

"Think this is where he was headed?" He gave a radio command to Jimmy to stay put, then turned back to Gracie.

"Yes. He ran toward the back of the church as if he knew where he was going. If he'd intended to use the front door, he could have seen it because of that pole light out front. The back window is an easy way in and out. I use it all the time."

"You *do?!* You're sure he's not armed?"

"Not sure, but I don't think so. He seemed very frightened. I doubt that's how he would be if he had a gun."

"You never know." Herb turned his radio volume way down and talked to Jimmy again.

Gracie watched and listened as best she could. She saw and heard nothing.

"By the way," Herb asked her, "where's the wallet?"

"The wallet! I dropped it. I must have dropped it, unless it's on the seat of my car."

He smiled. "Glad to see you're human. I was starting to doubt. But you made all the right moves, Gracie. Good girl."

"I had help."

Herb looked at her.

She pointed up.

Movement at the church's back window caught their eyes pretty much simultaneously.

Tensing, Herb suddenly changed from casual friend into police officer. The alteration was real, obvious, palpable. He cautioned, "Keep your head down."

Over the radio came Jimmy's voice, loudly. "Hey, chief. Don't shoot the guy in the back window. It's me."

Herb keyed his radio. "Who else is inside?"

"Roger and Maria. We secured the building. Nobody here but us cops. You can't imagine how many little nooks and crannies this place has. Just carefully checking all those rows of pews was a chore."

"So he got out before we arrived. I think Gracie just wasn't certain. Okay, Jimmy, close it down." Herb sat back and relaxed.

Herb swung the squad car around. "Gracie, you remember seeing anyone foreign-looking in the neighborhood?"

"What does that mean?"

"I'm not sure, just was hoping you'd know it if you saw it." He drove around to the front and parked next to Gracie's car.

Gracie got out because Herb got out. Something was nagging at the back of her mind.

With the other pair of Willow Bend's finest at his heels, Jimmy came out the front door. The woman officer locked it behind them.

"We found this on the stairs going up to the choir loft." Jimmy dropped a plastic bag containing something into Herb's hand.

Herb handed it to Gracie. "Amy's wallet?"

She grinned. "Yes it is."

"Found this, too." Jimmy gave him a second clear-plastic evidence bag. And in it was a knife with double-edged, six-inch blade.

"Where?"

"Bottom of those stairs that go up to the loft, on the carpet." Jimmy squared his shoulders. "Well, guess it's back to patrol, right, Chief?"

"Right. Thanks, guys. Appreciate it." He watched his officers get into their cars and leave.

"You didn't get a look at Jason at all?" Herb turned his attention back to Gracie.

"Not in good light." Gracie ran the mental tapes of those terrifying moments through her head again. "But I did see him slightly as he ran away down the hall. He gave me the impression that he's blond."

What she didn't say is how much less impression his appearance made on her than the poignant phrase he had uttered with such wretchedness, "My little boy is dying."

25

Terror sure does take it out of you. Gracie felt so tired, she knew that when she finally got to bed she wasn't even going to hear the pillow crumple.

Saying nothing about Jason Cates, the knife or even the police, she had taken the contents of Amy's wallet to her, explaining that the money had already disappeared from it and that the police had checked it for fingerprints.

Amy had thanked her profusely. The money was not as important to her as the rest of it, she reassured Gracie.

Then, as Herb had specifically asked her to, Gracie had returned not to her own but to his home, where she had left her car, anyway.

Rocky had arrived there in her absence, no doubt summoned by Herb. The three now sat around Herb's kitchen table drinking coffee and eating from a box of sugary doughnuts. "You can't be a cop without doughnuts," Herb joked.

Gracie was too weary to be polite. "Rocky, what are you doing here?" Normally grateful to see him on any occasion, she was, at the moment, uncertain of his allegiance. It was a new sensation and one she wasn't enjoying.

"Good question. Why am I here, Herb?"

"Because you know everything that's going on in Mason County. The FBI guys are messing this up. They have their own pet theories and just aren't looking at anything else. If this case is going to get resolved, I think it's you and I who are going to have to resolve it."

Rocky nodded at Gracie. "Then why is this lovely amateur here?"

"She's helping me, and I know she wants to find out what's going on, for the community's sake and not just for her own. She has a way of learning things we don't seem able to."

Gracie didn't know whether to feel flattered or exploited. She decided on the former.

Rocky refilled his coffee mug. "So it was Jason in the church with the knife. Sounds like a guess in a game of *Clue.*"

"Gracie believes it was Jason Cates and I'm trusting her instincts on this."

Rocky gave Gracie a quick thumbs up.

"Anyway, they had already grabbed the wife and held her for three hours but had to let her go. Her lawyer showed up."

"Wait," Gracie interrupted. "She can't afford a lawyer, can she?"

Herb grinned wickedly. "Friend of mine. He dropped by at my request and helped me out long enough to spring her. They had no reason whatever to detain her. Made me mad. She disappeared promptly, and they haven't been able to find her since. Not that they haven't tried."

"No wonder they looked so startled when they asked me when I saw her last and I said 'a couple days ago.' "

"You didn't take her out to lunch again, did you?"

"No." So Gracie explained how and when she had seen Hannah. She ended with, "I feel guilty. Why didn't we make a greater effort to reach out to her? We should have at least called out to her and asked to help."

Rocky stared at her. "You're serious, aren't you!"

"Why wouldn't I be? We saw her, right there. In the rain, no less. And we did nothing."

"Well, just put that little guilt trip to rest. She's a fugitive. She wasn't going to let you or anyone else get near her. Of course she ran the first time you saw her."

"The guilt stays. Jesus said to go out into the world, not wait for the world to come ask you. We failed to make an effort we should have made, whether she responded to it or not."

"If you say so." He poured himself another mug of coffee, obviously not caring if it kept him awake half the night.

Herb sat lost in thought a few moments. "If she's without a car, as she said, and if he's in town, as he obviously seems to be, they're probably holed up somewhere not far from the Eternal Hope Church."

"Or *in* the church," Rocky finished for him.

"Nobody there when my officers tossed the place. Gracie?"

"I doubt it. There's too much activity during the day. And when I was there after dark — I don't know, but I don't think there was anyone else there."

Rocky asked the obvious. "Then why was he there?"

Herb leaned forward. "Gracie, it seems to me you're in a key position here. You now are acquainted with both of the Cateses, and you have an ear open at the church. Whatever is happening, you can be

171

sure Eternal Hope is at the center of it, somehow."

Gracie tried to think, but she was too exhausted to do a good job of it. The idea that she was in any key position tended to frazzle her more. She liked a quiet life. The choir, keeping house, cooking, sharing with Marge an occasional catering job, walking, praying, reading: none of that meshed well with the notion of "key position" in any potentially dangerous adventures.

So why did she keep finding herself involved in them?

The conversation between the two subsided.

"Rocky?" She smiled sweetly at the editor. "You want an early scoop on any news, I assume."

"Got something for me?"

"Not yet, but the potential is apparently great. Herb? You want inside information, too, right?" Her voice dripped honey.

"Right. You're getting at something."

"Correct. What did you gentlemen intend to do for me in return?"

They both stared at her.

"I can see it hasn't occurred to you." Gracie paused, to gain greater effect. For now, she had forgotten her exhaustion. She was even enjoying herself.

"Herb," she then said, "this pertains to our investigation. With your police powers, will you please find someone for me?"

"Police powers. You kidding? I can't even find Jason Cates." He smiled. "But, sure, Gracie. Who?"

"The former treasurer of Eternal Hope. Bill Smyth."

Then she turned to Rocky. "You," she said. "You can take a break on leaping to ill-considered conclusions, such as considering Paul Meyer a criminal mastermind. What I want you to do is help me out with that ad. Okay?"

26

The wind coming off Lake Michigan was brisk. Beside Gracie, Carter Stephens, her niece, was dressed for the office and looked her usual capable self. Gracie smiled at Carter and knew she didn't need to express her gratitude any further. Gracie, after all, had a feeling that Carter enjoyed their adventures together even more than she did her official job. And, as jobs went, hers was a pretty official one: She was a lawyer in the office of the Cook County District Attorney.

Behind her, Rick Harding shifted his laptop case from one shoulder to the other. He muttered, "I hate Chicago."

Gracie turned to look at him. "I thought you were from here originally."

"There's only three good things about this place. You have your Field Museum, your Shedd Aquarium and your Berny's Ribs and Ale. After that, it's all downhill. You might as well live in a foreign country. Like Idaho, maybe."

Carter sniffed. "You are so grumpy when

you haven't had lunch, Rick."

Beyond them, north along the lakeshore, Grant Park invited those who would enjoy the museums and attractions or simply the views. Few lingered today in such blustery weather. Behind them to the south stretched Burnham Park, inviting in its own way.

They watched people entering and leaving Shedd Aquarium by the main doors before them.

Carter asked, "What makes you think he'll come out these doors instead of a side door? You said he was an employee, didn't you? They usually come and go by other ways. Or maybe he brown-bagged his lunch today."

"Early this morning, Herb Bower did some computer sleuthing and came up with a current place of employment for our former church treasurer. Shedd Aquarium. He's in their payroll office."

"I'm not sure I'll know him if I see him." Rick's voice rumbled menacingly even when he wasn't trying to be menacing. It was the main reason that Gracie had brought him today.

"I hope he shows up soon." Carter glanced at her watch. "In two hours and five minutes, I have to be in the Cook

County courthouse."

"I'll contribute to your taxi fare," Gracie said.

"Paying for a taxi isn't the problem. Finding one during lunch hour is."

"Isn't that he?" Gracie nodded toward a portly young man coming out the main aquarium doors.

"Gained weight, dyed his hair. Wasn't it lighter?" Rick asked behind her.

"Interesting," Gracie commented. "Why did he want to alter the way he looked?"

"Let's go," Rick urged.

The three of them fell in behind the unsuspecting Smyth. Rick moved in ahead of Gracie, striding along the avenue as if he were a native. Carter separated herself from Gracie by perhaps fifteen feet.

At the red light, converging and pausing, they all stood within three feet of one another. The light changed. Head held high, Smyth obeyed the *walk* signal, blissfully ignorant of the small parade following him and only him.

Rick and Carter dropped back a bit. Rick whispered, "Buckingham's."

Carter countered with, "Costigan's. Faster service."

They continued down the street and marched around the corner.

When Bill turned aside into Costigan's Cafeteria, Rick entered the door right behind him. Rick was behind him as he moved into line. Despite garnering some dirty looks, Gracie and Carter broke the line to step in right behind Rick. Carter then moved ahead of Rick. She was breathing down their quarry's neck.

Bill Smyth had never seen Carter, but it was quite likely that he could recognize Gracie, for she had served on the board with him. Would he know Rick? Probably, but soon it wouldn't matter.

He picked up a tray and flatware, gave Carter the slightest of cursory glances and chose a salad. Then he glanced at her again. Gracie peeked from behind Rick, a bit worried. Why was he so interested in Carter?

Silly Gracie! She's a lovely young woman, with the kind of quiet confidence men respond to. Of course he would give her a second glance, and a third and a fourth. He paid no attention to Rick or to anyone beyond Rick. Their plan was still safe.

When he paid for his tray and walked out into the dining area, Carter abandoned her tray for Rick to handle and stayed right behind Bill. What would they do if he chose too small a booth or table? Fortunately, he did not. Gracie watched them excitedly as she paid for all three trays.

There went Rick with his and Carter's trays.

Carter was introducing herself to their quarry, shaking hands warmly. Smyth beamed, pleased and surprised at his new acquaintance.

Rick joined them. Smyth's grin fled.

By the time Gracie had arrived at the table, Bill Smyth looked like a rabbit with one eye on a distant hole and the other on the hawk.

He stared at Gracie. And stared. "I know you."

"Yes, you do. Gracie Parks." Gracie set her tray down and seated herself in the chair opposite Smyth's tray. "Please sit down, Bill. We won't bite you."

Cautiously, he plunked himself down. "What's going on here?"

"Do you remember Rick Harding?" Gracie waved a hand. "Baritone in Eternal Hope's choir."

Rick nodded as he sat down at Gracie's right, looking grim. Gracie couldn't tell if it was because they had agreed beforehand that he'd act as "muscle," or simply because he was hungry.

Gracie waved the other hand as Carter

sat down at her left. "And I see our legal counsel already introduced herself."

"*Legal* counsel —" The rabbit clearly realized that the hole lay much too far away for safety. "Why? What?"

Rick paused to swallow a large bite of stew before he dragged his laptop out of its case.

He took a second bite. Then he declared genially, "It takes a few moments to boot up. Incidentally, Bill, it's good to see you again. You left Willow Bend in such a hurry that we didn't get to say good-bye."

Smyth's fear hardened into anger, at least on the outside. "In twenty seconds I call the cops. I don't know what you people think you're doing —"

"No, you won't," Carter purred. "Did you know that federal government agents are swarming around Willow Bend right now, looking for you? They just don't know your name yet. As soon as they do, you're in for it."

Bill suddenly forgot his lunch lay in front of him. He glared from face to face. Rick was eating with enthusiasm. He paused occasionally to poke at his laptop keyboard.

Gracie explained, "Surely you've seen the news, Bill. A tornado damaged our roof and revealed a huge cache of money."

"Yeah, I saw."

"Here it is." Rick turned the laptop so that Bill could see the screen clearly. "This is the spreadsheet Lester put together. There are the amounts you claimed were in our accounts. There are the bills you failed to pay and the other expenditures that weren't satisfied. And this — let me scroll across, there — this is the bottom line, what's missing. I'm surprised you converted it to cash, but the more I think about it, it was a brilliant move on your part. Can't get anymore liquid than cash, right?"

"I didn't! They were bank errors! The discrepancies were all bank errors!" Smyth stared aghast at the screen.

"No, Bill," Rick disagreed, "that won't cut it this time." His deep voice oozed menace. "Feel free to scroll around."

Bill stared not at the intimidating Rick or even at the delicious Carter, but at Gracie across from him. "Maybe I made an error or two, but this isn't my doing, I swear! This is terrible!"

"It gets worse." Gracie regretted choosing green beans. They were soggy. Too late now. "You see, the government people *assume* that loose cash has to be somehow associated with something highly illegal. Therefore, anyone connected to the cash is a suspect. Even our pastor. And me. And you."

Rick punched a couple keys. "Now you'll notice that the amount found in the attic, over ninety thousand, is more than the discrepancies in the books. So you had some little money-maker on the side. Or maybe a big one. Maybe that wasn't your only hidden treasure trove, even?"

Bill Smyth's complexion was now an ashen hue. Hoarsely, he asked, "What do you want?"

"The truth. How did the money get there?"

"No. I mean, what do you *really* want?"

Rick's tone of voice left no question about obedience or denial. "The truth. How did the money get there?"

"How do I know you're not going to hand me over to the cops?"

"You don't. And if you've committed a federal offense, we're not going to abet it by keeping quiet. That's why Miss Stephens is here. She knows federal statute."

Gracie added, "But if we decide to tell them what we learn, we'll tell you first that we're going to. Promise."

Bill Smyth, as anyone in the world could

tell, was scared witless. He shook his head, started to speak, stopped. Gracie finished off the horrid green beans and worked on the (obviously instant) mashed potatoes and meatloaf.

Bill took a deep breath. "You're not going to believe me."

"Chance it."

"I don't know anything about money in the attic. That's the part you won't believe. I admit, okay? that I skimmed a real little bit off the soft drink machine. Just a little. Small change. But the cash up there? No way."

"You can tell us how it got there, though."

"No. I really don't know. The first I heard about it was on the news." His harried glance again flitted from face to face. "The only people I ever saw go up there were the choir and Pastor Paul."

27

Thank You for the safe trip into Chicago, and for our success there. So now thank You for answering one question, at least. But where do we go from here, God?

Also, we ask Your hand in leading us safely home.

Gracie found some of her best prayer time behind the wheel of Fannie Mae. Was Rick praying too? He sat beside her, staring out the windshield at the world, or perhaps at nothing.

He spoke. "Bill was kind of irritating when he was involved in Eternal Hope, but I tried not to let the irritation show. Now I see why. Incidentally, congratulations on getting Herb to find him, Gracie. That was quite a coup."

"You were great to come with me, especially since you had to take the day off work. But it did solve some of our many puzzles. And thank you again for your help. Your very presence helped make the difference, I think."

"Hey!" He grinned. "I got two hours of work done, until my laptop's battery fizzled. It's not lost time."

"Look!" Gracie hit the brakes and pulled to the side of the highway as rapidly as she could and still do it safely.

Rick twisted around to look out the back window. "Who is that? Are we stopping to help someone?"

"If I identified her correctly, based on my one quick glimpse, we are about to render aid to an Alcohol, Tobacco and Firearms investigator."

"Huh?"

"And her name is Roberta Desmond." Gracie backed up along the shoulder until Fannie Mae sat twenty feet in front of the car with the hood up. She got out and walked back to the disabled vehicle. Was her instant identification right?

It was.

Roberta Desmond watched Rick and Gracie approach. "Do either of you have a cell phone? Mine isn't getting out." No longer clad in the starched attire of a professional investigator, Ms. Desmond looked almost human. The wind, nearly as strong here as it was in Chicago, had done playful things to her hair, and her blue jeans had grass stains on the knees.

Gracie said, "I didn't bring one."

Rick wagged his head. "Sorry. I forgot it this morning. I don't do mornings, as a rule."

Ms. Desmond sniffed. "I hear you. Neither do I." She waved a hand toward her car. "Apparently I don't do afternoons either."

Rick took off his jacket and Gracie extended a hand. He gave it to her. "So what happened?"

"I was going along, and clunk. I quit going. I need to call for a tow."

"I suggest," said Gracie, "that you transfer your things to my car and we'll take you into the next town. You can arrange for a tow there. In fact, if you're going back to Willow Bend, you're welcome to ride the rest of the way with us."

"I remember you now. You were at the lineup. I got the impression you didn't like me."

"I don't like being stonewalled when I ask legitimate questions." Gracie smiled. "But you personally? No, I never disliked you personally."

Ms. Desmond looked at her. "That's very charitable of you." She frowned some more at her car. "We're about, what? An hour from Willow Bend?"

"About, depending on traffic."

Ms. Desmond pondered the situation a bit longer. "The day is shot, but I have appointments starting pretty early tomorrow. I am not going to sit around waiting for the car to get fixed. Yes, Ms. Parks, if I may, I'd like to continue into Willow Bend with you."

Rick asked, "What about your car?"

"It's a rental. The company can handle it. I'll arrange the tow and let them take care of the rest."

Her acquiescence startled Gracie. She and Rick cast sideway glances at each other. Moments later, they were on the road again, the three of them. Rick gave up the front seat to Ms. Desmond. She protested only mildly before she took it. They continued into town in silence.

Gracie kept half an eye on the ATF lady as she drove. Something big was eating the woman. She glared at nothing, bit her lip, chewed her fingernails, and otherwise indicated extreme discontent. Did Rick notice it in the backseat? Gracie caught his eye in the rearview mirror. He made an "I sure don't know what's going on" gesture, with both hands.

The silence in the car was thick enough to support a running horse by the time they entered the outskirts of Willow Bend.

The town was of a size, Gracie reflected, that the outskirts were pretty much also the inskirts. "Where do you want us to drop you?" Gracie asked her extra passenger.

"At Mrs. Fountain's," Roberta Desmond answered her.

Trying to sound casual, with only a few blocks until their destination, Gracie posed another question. "Why in heaven's name did you go through all that business about a lineup? And then put one of the choir members in it?"

"That Lester Toomley or whoever?" Roberta Desmond shrugged. "He was on the list of people seen messing around the church. Same with the really old guy you said was your uncle. I guess the surveillance person watching the church didn't realize your Lester fellow was in the choir."

Rick grinned. "Lester sings behind Estelle Livett. She's big enough that nobody can see him. You just sort of have to assume he's there. Next time you attend, listen for a tenor. He's back there somewhere."

Ms. Desmond thought about that a moment and actually smiled. "That's cute.

You know, you guys are all right. You're human."

"Lester's the treasurer," Gracie explained. "He stops by the church every now and then on business."

"I thought the treasurer was someone named Smyth."

"He quit and left town. I guess the church directory isn't updated yet."

"Where's this Smyth now?"

Gracie panicked. What should she say? How much should she reveal?

But Rick simply replied, with studied offhandedness, "He didn't leave a forwarding address."

28

Gracie arose unusually late the next morning: six-forty-five. Trips to Chicago always wore her down, and she'd been exhausted even before that expedition had become necessary. By the time Gracie had dropped Rick off, returned home and resumed what was left of the day's many chores, it was well past her usual bedtime.

She heard the garbage truck in the alley, lifting the container and compressing its load. She interrupted breakfast and the loud morning news to go out and retrieve her empty trash can.

She dragged the can in out of the alley and stopped cold. "Gooseberry! What are you doing out here?"

The big striped orange cat meowed and arched against her shin.

Gracie scooped him up and scratched under his chin. "Had breakfast yet, big fella?"

"Meow."

"What would you like?" She carried him to the back door.

"Meow."

"We don't have any. How about cat food?"

"Meow."

And so, cat food it was.

She served Gooseberry's breakfast before she made her own, of course. Priorities.

She settled in beside Uncle Miltie with her cereal and looked at the weather map on the TV screen. Rain in the Northwest and in Maine, thunderstorms in Kansas, and nothing right here. Typical for this time of year.

"Weather's all screwed up," Uncle Miltie grumbled. "It's all those atomic tests."

"That was years ago."

"Ripple effect. You know. How a butterfly in Beijing flaps its wings and you get snow here."

"I never did understand that."

"Doesn't mean it can't be so."

"That's true." She wasn't sure he wasn't joking.

The moment Uncle Miltie finished and left the room, Gracie wolfed down the rest of her cereal, prepared to follow him, should he head off somewhere. Even if it wasn't an unexplained foray, she was anxious just to have a better idea of his movements. She wouldn't have Marge today, as she'd be at her shop, but, perhaps this time, Gracie would be allowed to skulk without being detained by overzealous federal employees.

The phone rang. Gracie answered.

It was Pastor Paul. "Can you stop by the church? We have a little problem here."

So much for trailing Uncle Miltie. "Certainly. In a few minutes?"

"Fine."

As she hung up, Gracie reflected on her minister's tone of voice. It didn't sound as if he were facing a huge, menacing problem, but neither did he seem as at ease as he usually was.

As she pulled into the church lot, she almost instantly noticed the vehicle with the license plate TOOTLE. What was the high school band director doing here? On second thought, she probably knew, at least in general. Was he apologizing, accusing, giving an exact accounting, or merely cutting a new deal? Perhaps he would take his soft-drink machine out altogether and then the church could get one of its own.

She went inside and waved to Pat Allen

as she passed the secretary's office. Pat did not look cheery.

She continued to Pastor Paul's office, knocked and stepped on in.

She smiled and said, "Good morning!" to Pastor Paul and to Phil Murphy.

Her pastor replied with, "Good morning, Gracie." Mr. Murphy did not.

Gracie drew up a chair beside the desk and sat down. "What can I help with, gentlemen?"

"Did you bring your key to the soft-drink machine?" the pastor asked.

"I don't have one."

"Pat has you on record as having been issued a key."

"Then there's an error. Unless —" Things began clicking into place.

The beleaguered pastor recited Mr. Murphy's charge of skimming, and quoted the brief news article to that effect. Gracie, having heard it already, paid more attention to her own thoughts.

When Pastor Paul paused for breath, and before Phil Murphy could jump in with a reiteration, Gracie asked, "Does the record show that Bill Smyth had a key?"

Pastor Paul frowned and picked up the phone. "Pat? Did Bill Smyth have a key?" He sat there in silence a while, glaring out the window. The morning's cloud cover had broken.

"Thank you." He hung up. "No record for Bill."

Gracie had by now framed a possible way to handle this. "Don't do this with me in the room. I'm a suspect and I shouldn't know what's going on. Privately, ask Pat if Bill acted as intermediary when that key was issued — you know, saying Gracie needed one and signing it out for me."

"What would he want with a key?"

"What would I want with one? I don't fiddle with the machine, I don't even patronize it." *But, dear Pastor, I think you just told me how Bill was able to pilfer from it.*

Phil Murphy fumed, "It's your civic duty to use that machine! All of you! The band needs everyone's support!"

And Pastor Paul lost his temper. "We are loyal supporters of the Lord Jesus Christ! The band is just going to have to take second place. Or third. I looked up the file on the drink machine, and it says my predecessor put it in at your request as a favor to you personally. Now you complain to us. If you think we're not assiduous enough in our support of the band, then put your machine amid more zealous supporters. But you'll not find more honest ones than those here."

Gracie bit her lip. This was definitely not the time to mention Bill Smyth's peccadillos.

She let them both fume for a few more moments, then dived in. "Mr. Murphy, what led you to think our church was such a good location, when we do not often use the hallway where it's located?"

"It seemed like a good choice at the time. But I certainly called that one wrong!" He glowered at her.

"But why that choice?"

"I should have picked a larger church. You know, a more prosperous one," he gibed.

Gracie tried to get an answer from a few other directions before the conversation ended. It proved impossible. When Murphy had left, Gracie's question was still dangling — and she thought it had been a pretty good one, too.

"I'm going to go talk to Pat a few moments." The pastor headed for her office.

"I'll be using the phone in the library." Gracie detoured into the library and dialed a familiar number. "Good morning, Judith. Is Rocky available?"

His gravelly voice was on the line in moments.

"Good morning, handsome and urbane editor. Can you speculate on why band-leader Phil Murphy would want to put his beverage machine in Eternal Hope when so many better locations are available?"

"Good morning, perspicacious lady. Let me get back to you on that. Are you home?"

"I will be in five minutes. I'm leaving the church."

"Call you there."

Gracie waved toward the secretary's office and left, tussling with herself about how much to tell Pastor Paul. Bill Smyth had admitted his misdeeds. Petty theft from the drink machine was not a federal offense, regardless of what the irascible Mr. Murphy might think. In essence, Gracie and her strong-arm team intended to honor that.

On the other hand, she meant to point the pastor in a direction he might go. Let him pursue the matter on his own. He and Pat could work it out. That is, unless the pastor actually turned out to be engaged in some illicit enterprise of his very own.

Why is life never simple?

With the living room television set blaring, Uncle Miltie was dozing in his favorite chair when Gracie got home. She left him undisturbed and was straightening up the kitchen when the phone rang.

"Hello, Gracie," Rocky said. "I think one reason Phil didn't put his machine somewhere else is that there aren't many places. The school board won't let them go into elementary and middle schools. He has the high school market covered already. Most of the large churches put their own in and reap a hundred percent of the profits. Stores and malls almost all have contracts with major distributors and the big cola companies. That leaves Eternal Hope and the other smaller, or unaffiliated locations."

"My goodness, you did a lot of research in a hurry!"

"I have a Rolodex the size of a tractor tire. Actually, it only took one call, to a distributor friend of mine. Why did you ask?"

"Curiosity. It's going to kill me one of these days."

"If you're anything like your cat, you'll have eight more lives beyond that. Something else I can learn for you?"

Gracie thanked him, reminded him of his responsibility for helping with the Eternal Hope ad, and hung up.

Very slowly, the loose ends were starting to come together. Now if Gracie could

196

only figure out which ends they were, maybe she could make sense of this puzzle.

Thank You, Lord, for the help You've given so far. We're probably getting someplace, though I certainly can't tell where.

Come to think of it, that still doesn't tell me why Mr. Murphy chose Eternal Hope as opposed to one of the other sorts of places Rocky mentioned.

Maybe she wasn't any further along than before, after all.

29

"It seems like Sunday rolls around just about every week." Marge climbed into the back seat of Fannie Mae. With Gracie driving and Uncle Miltie beside her, they were on their way to church. Marge and Gracie hurried in to change to their choir robes, leaving Uncle Miltie on his own, to dawdle as he wished, saying hello to friends.

Based on their performance at the previous rehearsal, the choir was going to have to excel as never before. Rehearsal had not gone well.

Gracie slipped into her robe.

Marge peeked out into the hall. "He's not around. Okay, spies. Report. Who followed Uncle Miltie?"

Lester announced, "While Gracie was up in Chicago, he left the house with that backpack. He walked up by the church and met another old man in the street. I didn't recognize the fellow but I have his description written down here. They talked awhile and then went together to the little pet store down on Fifth. I had to work in the afternoon, so I don't know where they went from there."

Amy reported, "He had a snack at Abe's. I was working behind the counter after school when he came in. He ordered his usual — blintzes and applesauce — and left in about an hour."

Don asked Gracie, "Are we getting anywhere with this? I realize we're pretty sporadic about following him around, but is there any indication at all that he's doing anything substantially out of the ordinary?"

Gracie sighed. "Good question. I guess it wasn't such a great idea. But I was so hoping to find out either what he's doing that seems to be bothering him or why he's acting so furtive. I thank you all for your efforts."

"Warm-up time." Barb Jennings seated herself at the piano. "Rick, hurry, please. Get in position. Very well, now, an A —"

Pastor Paul stepped inside the vesting room. "Has anyone here seen my sermon notes from last week?"

Barb looked displeased at the intrusion. After all, it was only the pastor. "About our financial situation? Or the sermon you would have delivered if you hadn't talked about that?"

"The one I gave, with facts and figures."

Everyone looked at each other, rather perplexed. All agreed that they had no idea what had happened to them.

Pastor Paul thanked them and left.

Marge frowned at Gracie. "Now what was that all about?"

Gracie shrugged.

"People, please! An A." Barb's fingers rolled up the keyboard, striking the chord.

Gracie participated with all her voice but only half her mind. Who in the world would want to filch the pastor's notes? And why?

They filed up the creaky stairs then, and took their places barely in time to sing the convocation. They did a fairly creditable rendering of the anthem, contrary to the job done at rehearsal. They joined in the congregational hymn with gusto and four parts.

All the puzzles tickling at her mind silently melted away. Gracie loved worshipping God in this way! She listened to Lester singing his part behind Estelle and let herself be amused, as always, at his invisibility.

Pastor Paul delivered a standard textual

sermon today. It was based upon that day's readings, so he hadn't simply warmed up the leftover from last week. He brought up the old saying that your character is defined by what you do when no one's looking. But he took it a step further, identifying honesty, an element of character, as what you do or don't do when you think you can get away with it. He tied it neatly in with the daily scripture and closed with a prayer for God's mercy on the nation as well as on the congregation.

With the closing hymn, Gracie added her own prayer for guidance and insight. As the congregation filed out and the choir members gathered their things, the issues baffling her once more returned to close in on her thoughts.

She was stepping from the last stair to the carpet when she nearly bumped into a worshiper — Harold Mayhew.

He studied the staircase behind her.

"Mr. Mayhew, good morning. Can I help you?"

"Uh, no, uh . . . just on my way out." And he left.

Gracie could not recall ever seeing the man in her church before, but then she could not see the rearmost pews from her choir seat. And he did not have to be a member to attend, nor would membership mean he had to participate in any of the activities that drew Gracie.

She took her time putting away her music and robe. Uncle Miltie was always slow about getting back to the car. When she left the building, only a very few cars remained.

What was going on over there at the far side of the parking lot? It looked like a wild argument, and she recognized all four of the arguers. Don Delano and Pastor Paul stood belt buckle to belt buckle with two of the agents who had interviewed Gracie, Joseph Patterson and Martin Grzbovsky.

Then, as Patterson stuffed Pastor Paul, literally, into the back of a sedan, Agent Grzbovsky told Don to back off and stay out of the way. Gracie couldn't hear any words, but the hand gestures made the message abundantly clear, even from across the lot. Grzbovsky slipped behind the wheel. The door slammed. The sedan roared away.

Low heels and all, Gracie raced out across the asphalt to Don. "Don! What in heaven's name is going on?!"

He seethed. "They just collared themselves a material witness."

"Witness to what?"

"They don't have to say. And the usual rule about producing a charge within forty-eight hours or letting him go doesn't hold with a material witness. They can detain a material witness forever."

"This is insane!" Gracie watched the car disappear down the road. "Isn't there some way to get him out?"

"Obtain a writ. That can take days. It's time to get a lawyer. Past time."

"And pay for one with what?"

Don sighed. "Good point." He brightened. "Maybe Carter can point us to one. She's Illinois bar, but she surely knows people around here."

"Good idea! You call her. I'll pursue some other possibilities." Gracie headed for her car.

Uncle Miltie wasn't there yet. Very well. The man could get home on his own. If you're eighty, she decided, you're grownup enough to do that. This time she had her cell phone with her.

She dialed. And waited. "Hello, Herb. Sorry to bother you, but. You know that lawyer you said you called upon for Hannah some days ago? We need him again."

30

Gracie was just cleaning up the breakfast residue on Monday morning when the doorbell rang. Uncle Miltie, perched as usual at the kitchen table, was in a particularly difficult mood. She didn't even bother to say, "I'll get it." She dried her hands and went to see who was there.

She swung open the front door, half expecting officers of some stripe to carry her away. "Carter!"

She hugged her niece enthusiastically and ushered her into the kitchen. "Did you have breakfast yet?"

"Not really. A yogurt and coffee on the road."

Gracie abandoned Carter and Uncle Miltie to their happy greetings and put bacon on to fry. She got out three fresh eggs, a potato and the bread for toast.

As Gracie bustled about, taking out a selection of jams and starting a fresh pot of coffee, Carter was exclaiming over the gray bristles that had so recently taken up residence over her great-uncle's upper lip. He, of course, was delighted to be making an impression on someone new, someone who not only wasn't insisting he stop being lazy and shave but who, in fact, told him how distinguished he looked.

Though Uncle Miltie's intention, in fact, was to take a razor to the mustache soon, he had certainly proved his point, which was to demonstrate that one was never too old to make an interesting change and give stick-in-the-mud pals a bit of a surprise.

"What time did you get up?" Gracie broke in on the mutual admiration society.

"Three. I woke up early, so why lie in bed?"

"I understand what brings you," Gracie said as she grated the potato for hash browns, "but I had hoped you would simply recommend a local lawyer's name."

Carter hauled Gooseberry up into her lap and began scratching the cat in all the necessary places. "After you and I hung up the phone yesterday, I was thinking, 'This is very weird. Officers and agents just don't do this kind of thing. Something else is going on.' So I called my boss to pick his brain. We came up with some ideas, and he said he'd cover for me today so I could come down."

Uncle Miltie grunted. "And just how much is all this going to cost us? Your boss is a pretty big gun."

"Professional courtesy. It's an interesting problem."

Gracie broke the eggs into the pan. "Over easy, right? I also talked to Herb Bower, the police chief, yesterday. He knows a lawyer friend who's willing to help, and that man said the same thing. The case is weird."

"It has been from the beginning," Carter agreed, "starting with the twister."

"Wicked twister." Gracie stuck the bread in the toaster.

"Sort of a step-twister. From what I read in the paper, the national weather service didn't even know it was coming. It touched down right here and went away again. Wicked step-twister." She laughed, and so did Gracie.

Uncle Miltie did not. "Hope you two are getting enough amusement from it." And he left the room disapprovingly.

Carter watched him. She looked at Gracie.

Gracie shook her head. "I don't know either."

As their conversation moved on to other more pleasant topics, Gracie made a fresh pot of coffee, making sure to leave plenty for Uncle Miltie.

Eventually, Carter laid her napkin beside her plate, and stood up. Gracie left the plate on the table. There are, she recognized, more important things to do in life than constantly to be tidying up in one's kitchen.

They were going out, astride white horses, their shining armor all neatly pressed, this time to rescue a fair gentleman in distress.

The first stop, logically, was the police station to see if Herb had contacted his friend yet.

Gracie parked and they entered the front door. Gracie fully expected the usual morning chaos that she knew reigned in the squad room as the week got started.

But it was quiet. Deadly quiet.

Gracie led Carter toward Herb's office.

"Uh, Mrs. Parks?" Jimmy addressed her. "I wouldn't go in there."

Gracie stopped. "Oh?"

Across the aisle from him, Maria said, "No, wait a minute, Jimbo. You and I wouldn't set foot in there for a million bucks. But Gracie Parks here's the one to

207

do it. They aren't going to sack her if she interrupts. Go, Mrs. Parks."

But Carter had moved over near the chief's door. She cocked her head. Obviously she was listening to something going on inside the office. Putting a finger to her lips, she very cautiously turned the knob.

As she opened the door just a crack, the sound became intelligible.

Roberta Desmond was nearly but not quite shouting. "— don't have enough to arrest anyone! Until we do, all you're doing is signaling that we're on our way!"

"We have enough!" Grzbovsky's voice insisted. "At least we will when a couple of these yokels come clean for us. The time to strike is now, before they skip town."

They then began to upbraid one another, using terms that made Gracie blush. Meanwhile, the happiest smile had spread across Carter's face. She listened, occasionally nodding. And then she very carefully closed the door again. She stepped over to Jimmy's desk. "Ring the phone in there for me, please."

Grinning, Jimmy punched in an extension and handed the receiver to Carter.

She stood there a moment. Her voice lilted. "Ah, good morning, Chief Bower. This is Carter Stephens." Pause. "Fine,

fine, thank you. Couldn't be better. And yourself? Good! Say, I'm in your squad room out here listening to the racket. Can I invite you to join us for coffee? It sounds like you could use some." Pause. "Yes it does." Pause. "Good!" She handed the receiver to Jimmy and he cradled it.

Chief Bower came out of his office moments later, and not in a good mood. He glanced at Gracie. "It figures. You're coming to coffee too, I suppose."

"You sound disappointed." Gracie fell in beside him as he and Carter headed for the door.

"Naw, it's just that you're part of a major conspiracy extending from here clear into South America, and I don't know if I'm ready to hobnob in circles so powerful."

"To Bolivia, specifically," Gracie suggested.

He looked at her. "Yeah." They stepped out into the clear and blissfully quiet streets of Willow Bend.

Carter said, "To encapsulate what I heard in there, the feds think that this town is somehow the hub of a huge organization of some sort extending into South America. Drug-runners, I would presume."

"Arms traffickers."

"Okay, arms traffickers. Despite the fact that most of the arms in this town are twenty-gauge shotguns belonging to weekend hunters, who shoot at rabbits and ducks with them. That means that you are surely a major suspect, having the town's primary enforcement role. How did you escape?"

"I didn't. I don't think they meant to start squabbling out loud in front of me. I learned some things, though, from what they let slip."

"Like what?" Gracie asked.

"They're pretty sure that this traffic is somehow centered in Eternal Hope Church. Crack the pastor and you've got one of the middlemen, at least. That means that all the church members are suspects."

Carter arrived at the little convenience store across the street ahead of Herb and Gracie and laid a twenty on the counter. "For all of us," she said.

Her companions didn't argue. They gave their orders, accepted their coffee, and headed for the benches outside.

"See if you can make any sense out of this." Herb sipped. "The problem seems to be that everyone smiles and waves to everyone else. Everyone seems to *know* everyone else. Gracie, you were telling Ms. Desmond all about Chuckie Moon, when he didn't go to your church or anything. That's an example Ms. Desmond gave."

"But everyone does know everyone in Willow Bend!"

"I see!" Carter nodded. "But not in big cities, and these people are big-city oriented. So since everyone meets everyone else's eye when they're out in public, and maybe even chat with strangers, they're obviously all in it together. It's just all one big conspiracy."

"That's how I read it, but I wasn't sure I could trust my own opinion." He looked slyly at Gracie. "Now your lover is —"

"My lover?! Who —"

"Rocky Gravino, of course. Since he controls the press, which is the first thing you have to control, he's probably pretty close to the top. Ouch! Hey!"

Gracie had set her coffee down, a precaution, before kicking him smartly in the shin.

"Way to go!" Carter grinned.

Herb scowled. "They talk about Rocky being employed by Eternal Hope, even though he's an atheist! They assume that it's hush money or something similar. Can you fill me in on that at all, Gracie?"

211

Gracie picked up her cup again. "Lester Twomley asked him to make a guess as to how much it would cost to repair our roof, based on his experience reporting estimates. There were no payments. He did it as a freebie."

"Ah. Pretty smart. This is why I engaged you as a spy, you know."

"And he's not an atheist. He's an agnostic."

"Whatever. But if it's a conspiracy they want to investigate," Herb grumbled, "let 'em look at women. Every woman in the world is a member." And he reached down and rubbed his shin.

31

Gracie sat on the glider on her porch sipping her tea. Resting. Just resting. Active days left her more in need of rest now than they once did, and the need seemed to begin earlier in the day. She had just seen Carter off with thanks and hugs, wishing her a safe journey home.

Was the machinery that Carter, along with Herb's friend, had set in motion sufficient to spring Pastor Paul? Tomorrow he would be out at noon if it was. If not, Gracie had no idea what to do next. This problem lay beyond her province. If what she'd tried didn't work, others must solve it.

She did not rest for long. Too many tasks called, their irresistible urgings prodding her back into action. For one thing, she was overdue in writing a newsy letter to her son Arlen, who lived in New York with his family. They talked most weeks, but she still enjoyed the old-fashioned discipline of gathering her thoughts and putting them on paper.

Often it even helped her see better what was going on in her life and in Willow Bend if she shared it with Arlen, who'd grown up there but lived away for so long.

When the letter was finished, she was faced with a choice. She could go in and start dinner, or she could drive over to Eternal Hope and trim up the church hedge there, which she usually did. She decided dinner could wait an extra forty-five minutes. Leaving a note under a fridge magnet for Uncle Miltie, she tossed her clippers onto the seat beside her and drove to the church.

On the way, she pondered the inscrutable differences between the city turn of mind and small-town attitudes.

Look at the misunderstandings that resulted from those subtle differences. They were certainly no one's fault specifically, but how they caused problems!

She parked near to the church hedge and got busy.

Eventually she needed more sheer altitude than she possessed. Pat had gone home by now, so she used her key to get inside. She borrowed the stepstool from the warden's closet to trim the last of the hedge.

Standing on the stool, she clipped away — and hesitated briefly — then clipped some more, trying to pretend she had not been taken aback. Was that not movement she'd seen through the window? Maybe it wasn't. The sky's light reflected so strongly on the glass that seeing anything was difficult.

Stretching and reaching, she finished up the back of the hedge on top, then went inside again to return the stool.

She saw no one in the library or in Pat's office. But she heard a male voice, and it was coming from the front room. She recognized it as belonging to Jason Cates.

"No," he was saying. "I tell you there isn't any money. No." Pause. "I don't know. I'll work it out somehow."

Silence.

I feel bold, Lord, or perhaps foolhardy. I hope this is Your doing and that You are with me now.

She stepped into the doorway. "I thought I heard a voice in here."

Jason Cates jumped straight up. He stared. "You're Gracie." He relaxed the slightest bit and settled back into the chair by the reading desk. "I thought everyone was gone."

"Everyone was. I just came over and

trimmed the hedge." She leaned against the jamb.

"I don't have a phone, so I came in to borrow this one."

The young man mused bitterly, "If only we'd never gone down to Bolivia . . ."

What could she reply? Nothing.

He stood up. "So are you going to run and tell the police you saw me here?"

"To what purpose?"

"I'm stealing the use of your phone, for starters."

"You need it. We have it. Would Jesus refuse you use of His phone? I doubt it. We don't begrudge it."

"The police want me."

"Do they? They haven't asked me to find you. They haven't even published the fact that you're a fugitive. If they need help, the very least they can do is ask for it."

And the same goes for you, Jason Cates. You need help. But until you ask me, what can I do?

"I hadn't thought of it that way." Here he came across the room toward her.

She felt an instant's panic, but she maintained her casual slouch. He walked past her and headed down the hall toward that window.

He had not turned on any lights and by

216

now the room was nearly dark. She let herself out the front door and got in Fannie Mae. And immediately locked the doors. No use taking chances, though she wasn't at all certain of who or what she was frightened.

Please, Lord! I'm not sure what seeds I planted, but I do want to help him, and his family as well. Lead me, here. I beg You.

It was nearly dark when she got home. Still, Uncle Miltie, the mysterious wanderer, came in five minutes behind her.

Tomorrow, she really must follow him!

32

"Good. Now that you're on-line, you click up here on *Find* and type *Bolivia* in the box. See?" Amy Cantrell pointed to the screen. "You can go anywhere in the world you want to and never leave your chair. Even unsafe places."

Dutifully, Gracie scooted the pointer where told, clicked, typed *Bolivia* and hit Enter. The screen went blank. "Now what did I do?"

"The right thing." Beside her, Amy giggled. She seemed to be having more fun with this tutorial on the church's computer than Gracie was. Amy looked as angelic in jeans and sweatshirt as she did in a choir robe on Sunday.

With slow and elegant casualness, the screen began to paint a list of options. It took a long moment as first one element came on view, and then another.

"Now I choose?" Gracie tried to read the rather small print rapidly.

"Right. And if you don't think what you

see is useful, type in something slightly different, for another try. See where?"

"Yes. There's an awful lot of information here."

"My dad says, 'So many facts, so little wisdom.' But it sure is great when you have to do a term paper in a hurry. You can download and print pictures, even."

With a sort of morbid fascination, Gracie clicked and pointed and clicked again, discovering the world. El had died before the Internet became the casual tool of the average teenager. What would he say to this? Probably the same thing that Amy's father said.

And then Barb called for choir rehearsal to begin. Amy showed Gracie how to end the program and shut down.

"Can we practice in the sanctuary tonight, please?" Amy asked Barb. Others concurred. Gracie gave her vote for downstairs just because it was what Amy wanted.

Barb reluctantly gave in and they assembled near the altar.

She shuffled her music. "All right, my friends, we have a new one tonight." She ignored the responding groans. " 'Fight the Good Fight,' E-thirty-two. There's no chorus in this one, so we'll vary the key on four. I'll play it through." And she seated herself at the piano.

What had Gracie learned in her swift sortie upon the web? She learned that U.S. troops had gone to Bolivia in the mid-1980s to try to help the local government curb the traffic in cocaine. The country was, it appeared, a major producer. Of its legitimate output, though, very little was in manufacturing or electronics. Most was agricultural. The major portion of the nation's roads were not completely paved. Their unit of currency, the Boliviano, equalled about fifteen or twenty American cents.

So many facts, so little wisdom, indeed.

She wondered most of all about Jason Cates. Traveling the length of the hemisphere seemed like such a casual thing to him. Her own contact with and knowledge about Bolivia came solely from the Internet. Virtual experience was all it was, whereas Jason had actually driven its dusty roads, eaten in its restaurants, and possibly had even encountered an Andean llama or two.

Amy, for her part, seemed to think that the virtual was as good as the real.

Not at all, Amy! Not at all.

"Stop." Sighing dramatically, Barb

closed her eyes. "Estelle, I know you like to trill the high G, but here it is simply not appropriate. All right, starting with the second verse." She raised her baton.

In Pat's office, the phone rang. You could just hear it. Gracie had the strongest urge to answer it, but she kept her seat. On the fourth ring the answering machine picked it up and no doubt informed the caller of office hours. The rehearsal continued unbroken.

Gracie was letting her thoughts wander too much! She tried to apply herself more vigorously to the music. Unfortunately, her mind had a mind of its own and kept going back to the Bolivia conundrum. What was ringing false? What was tickling so persistently at the back of her rebellious brain?

Aha! She got it. Unfortunately, it only generated more thinking and still robbed her attention from the rehearsal. This, *not* thinking about Bolivia, was her job of the moment. But she enjoyed only partial success at keeping her attention fully upon the music.

They finally mastered the chording of the third line of each of the stanzas and were about to get on with the finale when Don Delano leaped to his feet and started to clap and cheer. So did Amy and Marge. Lester stood up simply to see what was happening. And then Gracie jumped up clapping as well.

For here came Pastor Paul down the center aisle! He had not shaved since Sunday and he looked altogether disheveled, but what else might one expect from a prisoner just now set free?

He hugged and shook hands with all present. Gracie noticed that Barb hid her irritation amazingly well, considering her usual hostile reaction to anything that interfered with precious practice time.

"When did you get out?" was Lester's first and most obvious question.

"About an hour ago. They finally decided nothing was going to happen."

"Why didn't you call us?" Don asked.

"I did. No one answered." Paul was still grinning. "It's a short walk. No problem. Believe me, I needed the exercise." He waved a hand. "You guys finish up. I'm just going to pull down my e-mail and then go home."

He walked away to his office and Barb rapped sharply on her music stand. Back to work.

Mercifully, half an hour beyond the usual quitting time, Barb called a halt. She wearily gathered up her scores and left the sanctuary.

"Don?" Gracie waved him down. "May I speak to you a few minutes?"

"Sure!" He walked beside her to the vesting room to file their music.

"Tell me everything you know about cocaine and heroin."

He looked startled a moment, then grinned. "And what makes you think I'd know anything about drugs?"

"You teach science, don't you? Of course you know everything about them."

He paused and nodded. "Actually, I don't know much about anything drug-related except the basic chemistry."

"Where's it grown? Don't you at least know that?"

"Well, that's easy — anywhere drug entrepreneurs can get away with it. Mostly, I think, southeast Asia and South America."

"Have the sources shifted, do you know? Like, from one part of South America to another?"

"I have no idea. It's just not anything I've ever studied."

Gracie perched on the edge of her chair. "I'm sure there are other things I should be asking, but I don't know what they are. And neither do you. Thank you, though,

Don. Can I treat you to ice cream?"

"I'd love it, but I have papers to grade." He stood up. "Call me when you think of something else to ask, that I might know more about."

Being the last ones out, they locked up. He accompanied her out to Fannie Mae and drove out of the lot right behind her.

Silly, to lock up the front door when Jason and I and who knows who else can enter so handily from the back.

Now, God, first of all I thank You again, as I have repeatedly already, for bringing Pastor Paul out of jail and back to us. I praise Your name!

Also, tonight I have learned lots of things and none of it makes much sense. Or maybe it does. At any rate, thank You so much for creating such an interesting puzzle!

33

By the time Sunday again popped up on Gracie's calendar, she still had not been able to track the comings and goings of Uncle Miltie. Things kept coming up to interfere with her plan, and the rest of the choir seemed to have abandoned the idea. She spent a good day and a half simply helping Pastor Paul get caught up in his office. And in that time she learned not a stitch of anything interesting or subversive to relay to her spy supervisor, Herb.

Gooseberry was still behaving peculiarly at times. In short, nothing had changed.

Sunday morning, Gracie donned her robe and performed all the functions of being a choir member, and gratefully. This was a very pleasant service to her Lord.

The anthem went about as it had been rehearsed, which is to say, there were some rough spots. During it, Estelle decided that to trill the high note was the thing to do after all, incurring Barb's wrathful glare.

In his message, Pastor Paul addressed

the commonly held misconception that you earn your way to heaven with good works. Gracie might have wished that her personal federal agent was listening, but she hadn't seen him lately.

Then Paul turned the idea around and showed his congregation the back of it. "If you are committed to Jesus, you are going to heaven. And if you are committed to Him, you are going to do what's right and not wrong. That's not in order to earn heaven. Rather, it is in gratitude because He's bringing you there. My friends, we owe Him everything. Everything!" He then went into the crowns and jewels in crowns — but the main message was what Gracie focused on, since all too often she knew she lost sight of it.

Afterwards she headed to the vesting room with the others to put away her things. She happened to glance back up the hall and stopped.

Harold Mayhew was starting up the choir-loft stairs.

Gracie left her music on a chair just inside the room and hurried down the hall. It was impossible to sneak up those noisy wooden stairs undetected, but if she took a step when he did, perhaps he wouldn't notice.

It worked. The two of them squeaked their way upward in unison. Gracie stopped when he topped out. She was far enough up the steps behind him that she could see him well.

He proceeded directly to that torn-apart cubbyhole and stood there a moment. Then he knelt in front of it and crossed himself! Was he muttering a prayer? Gracie's ears could not tell.

As he was standing up, he twisted and saw her before she could duck. She watched anger waltz across his face. But it quickly faded.

She was discovered. She might as well indulge her clamoring curiosity. She continued to the top of the stairs. "I'm sorry I spied on you. I thought I saw someone coming up here and wasn't sure."

"Got your eyes and ears full, I bet." He scowled not at her, but at everything except her.

"No. Which makes me all the more curious."

He looked at her then. "You look kind of like a priest with that robe on, you know."

"I can't imagine that. I certainly don't feel like one. You were raised as a Catholic, I take it."

He grunted. Then he unexpectedly

smiled. "Clear back to Mary Queen of Scots. Did you know that? My aunt traced our family clear back to there on the Mayhew side. My mama's side was poor Irish, but not the Mayhews. That's a long time to be a Catholic, ain't it?"

"It's a glorious heritage."

"Yeah. Yeah, it is." He looked at the cubbyhole one last time and sat down in Lester's chair. So Gracie drew Amy's chair over beside him and sat down as well.

"Want to hear a crazy story?" he asked. "Goofy old-man stuff?"

"Yes, I do."

"To start with, I don't know why I came here last week. The only two times I ever went to church were my wedding and my wife's funeral. But I came. Mostly just curious, I guess. Your preacher talked about character, remember? And honesty. About how the measure of your character is what you do when nobody sees you. And honesty is doing the right thing even if you could get away with the wrong thing."

Gracie marveled. He certainly remembered the text better than most of their congregation did. She said nothing, merely letting him continue.

He did. "That got me. I mean, really got me. Punched me in the stomach. Here I am a descendant of royalty, and trying to get by with cashing in after bald-faced lying. To a church, yet! No more of that, I decided. It's time I shaped up. So this week I came back, and your preacher got me again. Now he's saying you can't earn your way to heaven."

"Another punch in the stomach?"

Harold chuckled. "I thought it was a pretty good idea, myself. Gave you something to work for, you know? But the idea that you do it because you're thankful — I think I like that even better."

"You were coming up the stairs last week, but when you saw me you changed your mind. Is that correct?"

"That's correct. More goofy old-man stuff." Harold scratched his stubbly chin. "Right after the sermon ended, I sat there knowing what I'd have to do. Quit lying. And I hated to, but I was certain. Determined, I mean. So I was going to come up here and say good-bye to the place. I mean, this is where they found all that money that was never mine, and now it's never going to be."

He sounded so sincere and eloquently repentant that Gracie could only say, "That's very beautiful."

"Beautiful?!" He laughed. "Not from

this crazy old geezer."

"No, not from a crazy old geezer. You're right. But from a descendant of royalty, it's lovely." And then a remarkable thought struck her and tickled her breastbone. "Harold, do you know who the son of Mary Queen of Scots was?"

"James the First of England. I think he was James the Fifth or Sixth of Scotland."

"And you're familiar with the King James version of the Bible."

He stared at her.

She nodded. "Same James. Now that's a heritage to take pride in!"

He beamed. "Imagine that. Never thought of it. Gracie, *you're* a queen!" And he hopped to his feet. "Now I got plenty to live up to. Thank you, m'lady!" With a final wave to that empty cubbyhole, he bounded merrily down the old rickety stairs away from the silent choir loft and back out into the cold, demanding world.

34

The television set blared the evening news as Gracie cleaned up the supper dishes. She was still amazed and a bit dumbfounded by Harold Mayhew's awakening. *All that happened Sunday night, Lord. Does that mean that Harold will abandon his claims? Or did the feeling fade the day after, today, Monday? I pray You'll accept and direct his soul, regardless of the money business! That's not the important part. Harold is.*

It was raining again. Gracie thought of Hannah and hoped she and her children were safe and dry somewhere. How she wished she could help. At least, she decided, wind and tornadoes were not a part of the picture this time.

Gracie heard Uncle Miltie call, "I'm leaving." Anyway, she thought that's what she heard. She dried her hands and went out into the living room.

The newscaster onscreen was talking again about federal funds set aside for a massive crime-fighting effort. Hadn't they been talking about that weeks ago? Did it still rank as news? Apparently there weren't as many millions available as the relevant agencies had originally hoped. That didn't strike Gracie as newsworthy either. There never *are* enough.

Somewhere beyond the closed front door, Gracie thought she heard Gooseberry meow. Had the cat started to go with Uncle Miltie and changed his mind? Gracie opened the front door to let him back in. His canes clacking on the pavement, there was Uncle Miltie out to the sidewalk already and headed up the street past Marge's with his backpack. He had on his slicker with the hood up.

Gracie was going to call, "It will be dark in half an hour," but she decided not to. He was old enough to tell when the sun was setting without her help.

She thought she heard Gooseberry meow again, but he wasn't on the porch. He wasn't in his favorite position crouched under the shrubbery, either. But it was raining. She closed the door. He could take care of himself, too.

Now a female anchor was trying to be dramatic about an apartment fire that had amounted to nothing more than a blackened kitchen. Slow news day. Gracie turned the set off.

The phone rang as she entered the kitchen. She scooped it up on her way to the sink. "Hello?"

It was Marge. "I never thought I'd say this, Gracie, but let's go follow Uncle Miltie even though it's raining. He just went past my house."

Marge was right: Now was the time. Gracie neglected to mention that she knew Uncle Miltie had just left. "I'm on my way."

Hastily she grabbed her own slicker out of the hall closet. She donned her slip-on rainboots and pulled the little folded rainhat from her purse as she hurried out the door. She just barely remembered to lock it behind her.

She saw Marge through the mist ahead and jogged to catch up to her. They watched Uncle Miltie as he four-legged his way doggedly through the thickening drops.

Marge muttered, "I just love subjecting my body to climatological abuse this way. And I've been fighting a cold for two days, too. I must have eaten a tree-full of oranges."

They watched him pause at the curb, then cross the street.

Marge sniffed wetly. She was a trouper, but that cold she was fighting just might be winning. "It's going to be dark soon. Where does he think he's going?"

"I thought that was what we're trying to find out."

"This is insane."

Gracie couldn't have agreed more.

In the fading light they could just about follow Uncle Miltie by ear as he clicked his way down the street.

Gracie left the private-eye work to Marge for a few moments while she looked behind them. Were there still federal agents of some sort tailing them? Or had they given up on following a couple of old ladies who mostly went to choir practices?

She saw no cars, no furtive men in trench coats, sunglasses and fedoras. She saw no one at all.

When she turned forward, she didn't see Uncle Miltie, either.

Gracie and Marge stopped to hide behind a light pole, stretching their necks to see. Then Gracie hurried up the alley to the hedge and squeezed in. Marge came hustling in behind her. Cautiously they peeked out.

"I knew it!" Marge hissed.

"Ssh!"

Marge lowered her whisper. "He's headed straight for that vacant house on the alley corner behind the church. I knew it! I just knew it." They ducked back as Uncle Miltie twisted to look this way and that, up and down the alley.

Gracie allowed him a moment while he made certain no one was following, then peeked out, very carefully. He was turning his back to them again, lurching forward on his quad canes.

But he did not continue to the house. He turned aside and disappeared beyond the little cement-block garage behind the house.

Gracie hastened forward. Her plastic slip-on boots had sprung leaks, both feet. They were temporary boots, made for getting from the shopping mall to your car in the parking lot, and not for trooping all over town following a stubborn old man with a backpack. Her tennis shoes were getting soaked. She might have to enlist in Marge's battle against upper respiratory infections.

She would be detected if Miltie decided to come out to the alley and look around again. It was a risk she had to take. Her boots slipping and squooshing around on her feet, she broke into a jog.

He must have entered the garage

through its side door. She moved in closer, listening for any sound at all that would betray his presence. Should she peek in the window? No. The windows were too dusty to see through, even if there were enough light inside to show anything. And if she did, her head would show, detectable from the inside in silhouette, for it was still lighter out here than in there.

Marge's eyes got wide. "Voices!" she barely whispered.

Voices they were. But how to find out what was happening? Gracie tried to make out identities. She could not even make out words. Perhaps there was some way to hear better or even see on the other side of the garage.

And then Marge very quietly said, "Uh. Uh."

Oh no! Gracie quickly pressed the side of her finger to the base of Marge's nose where it connected to the lip.

"Uh . . . uh-*choo!*" Marge muttered, "Sorry."

Ah, well. Their cover was blown for sure now. Literally.

So Gracie walked over and knocked politely on the door.

35

The voices inside the little garage had fallen quite still.

Gracie waited. Marge blew her nose, since there was no longer a need for silence.

The door squeaked as it opened a bit.

Uncle Miltie's face appeared in the gloom beyond. "Thought it'd be you. You might as well come on in." He moved aside, his backpack in his hand.

With that warm welcome, Gracie and Marge stepped inside. A realtor would undoubtedly boast of this as a two-car garage, but it was actually a car-and-a-half at most. And, in fact, most of it was filled with a car. A junker younger than Fannie Mae, *sans* hood, doors and wheels, sat on cement blocks. The only light came from a window on each side, and with the rain, plus dusk upon them, that was almost none at all.

Hannah and her two boys cowered motionless in a corner. Both boys were frail and blond, with their father's wiriness.

When she spotted the three, Gracie should have said something tender and sweet. Instead she was suddenly gripped by anger, and she almost didn't rein it in in time. "That day in the rain, I wanted to help you!" she heard herself say. "Why wouldn't you let me?"

"Because they're fugitives!" Uncle Miltie exploded. "They didn't do a thing wrong. They're innocent, decent people. But they're fugitives! They can't leave this place. They can't show their faces in public. The boys can't go to school. That's why she didn't hang around and be nice to you."

"Yes, but . . ." And then Gracie saw Gooseberry.

The cat lay happily limp in the arms of the smaller boy, lapping up attention. Even in his wide-eyed fear, the child was automatically scratching Gooseberry's chin.

Suddenly Marge and Gracie ceased to be the center of attention. Hannah, the boys, and Uncle Miltie, as well, were staring terrified at the door.

Gracie wheeled. "Rocky!"

Rocky walked in and closed the door behind him. "Show me a good news reporter and I'll show you an inveterate snoop." He

238

looked at the three fugitives. "Me llamo Rocco Gravino, a sus ordenes. Y ustedes?"

The taller and obviously bolder lad replied, "Tim, a sus ordenes. Mi hermano se llama Bradley." He wrapped an arm protectively around his little brother's shoulders.

"Y tu padre? A donde esta tu padre?"

"No se. No sabemos, señor."

Gracie recognized the language as Spanish, but she didn't know what was being said.

Now that her eyes were as adjusted as they were going to get, Gracie looked around some more. She recognized her leftovers containers in the one corner. And she realized belatedly that this old auto served as the Cateses' bedroom. The tail of a blanket was sticking out of the passenger side. She had a blanket just like that at home in a closet. Or perhaps she didn't anymore. She recognized a couple of very familiar items in addition to Gooseberry.

And then Marge said, "Stop. Everyone here speaks English and only half of us speak Spanish. So switch over."

Rocky explained, "It was kind of a test. I wanted to know if these people really have been in Bolivia recently. They have. I also wondered if the boys had seen their father recently. They haven't."

Hannah still seemed very wary of Rocky — of Marge and Gracie too, for that matter. "Is it all right if I feed the boys?"

"Of course!" Gracie appreciated the miracle that was mothers all over again. No matter what the circumstances, they remember their flesh and blood. "I assume that dinner for three is in Uncle Miltie's backpack there."

"That's right!" Uncle Miltie negotiated his crippled body to the floor and opened his pack of goodies.

Hannah wielded a can opener Gracie recognized as being her spare from the back of her drawer. When she was checking for missing food, it had not occurred to her to scan for missing kitchen utensils as well. Maybe she would have put this puzzle together sooner.

Uncle Miltie had been shopping. Here were cans of beef stew, which Gracie never used, and a brand of canned fruit Gracie didn't normally buy.

The boys ate the stew cold, out of the cans. With gusto. Hannah received her own can. She sat down with a plastic spoon and dug in.

Uncle Miltie brought out three cans of soda and, popping the tops, handed them around. Gooseberry made it abundantly clear that any little morsel extended his way would not be out of line in the least. No one offered, however — they were too hungry themselves.

Rocky sat down in the open door of the junked car, his elbows on his knees. "Gracie, the next time you tell me about missing leftovers, I'll pay closer attention."

Gracie chose as her seat a carton that looked fairly sturdy. It sagged under her weight, but not seriously. "How long have you been following me? Marge and I didn't know we were coming until moments before we ran out the door."

"I wasn't, until you ran out the door, as you say. I was coming by with the proofs for that display ad just as you left. When I saw you two hoofing it up the street, I figured something was afoot here, excuse the pun."

Marge wrinkled her nose. "It looked that unusual?"

"In the rain, Marge?"

She shrugged and found her own carton to sit on.

"No, you weren't bringing ad proofs," Gracie contradicted. "You ran our ad already, and it didn't result in very much. Not enough that we can afford another one, at any rate — even a reduced one."

Did Rocky look ashamed? Possibly. Contrite? Definitely. "Listen, Gracie, I've been rethinking this whole thing. When you look at it objectively, your pastor's kind of an awkward guy but he made all the right moves for a man who needs money desperately while sticking to legal avenues. And when the feds jailed him and then turned him loose, he headed right back to the church and took up his duties and preaching."

"How do you know?"

"I dropped in for the early service on Sunday, just to see what he'd say. Also, he didn't hire a lawyer. That says something, if you know what I mean? So I already have put together a new ad for you to look at. See what you think."

"Wait!" Hannah looked shocked. "They put your pastor in jail?"

Gracie would have tried to say something that made it sound less harsh, but Rocky spoke before she could. "Material witness. They're looking for your husband and you."

Hannah closed her eyes. She looked incredibly sad. "It just keeps getting worse and worse. Every time I think maybe there will be an end somewhere, it gets worse.

We never should have gone to Bolivia in the first place."

Only Gracie knew she was echoing her husband's exact sentiments.

"It's not your fault," Marge reminded her.

"But it's all because of me! Because of us. That's just as bad." Gooseberry curled against her shin, arching his back with affection.

"Why did you go to Bolivia, of all places?" Gracie asked.

"A job offer. A company asked Jason to go down there and be a troubleshooter for some specialized equipment. The salary was amazing. They paid for all of us to go, so we moved down there."

"What was the job, exactly? I mean, after you arrived." Rocky shifted a little. His seat couldn't be very comfortable.

"Fixing things, like they said. And mechanical work on trucks. Jason's very good at it, and he enjoys it. He liked the variety, with a different problem every day. A few months later, Jason was asked to go out in the field to work on some machinery. When he came back he was just horrified. 'This outfit's a drug operation,' he said. 'They grow the stuff.' So we started saving as much of his paycheck as we could, and when we had enough for the tickets, we walked out one day, drove to the airport and got on a plane. Everything we took down there we left behind — the boys' toys, everything — but it was worth it."

Rocky asked, "How much cash did you bring back with you?"

"About twelve hundred bolivianos. We exchanged it for American money when we got here."

"That's only about two hundred dollars!" Gracie exclaimed.

As one, Marge and Rocky and Uncle Miltie said, "How would you know that?" The only ones not surprised were Hannah and the boys.

"The immediate question before us is," Uncle Miltie reminded all of them, "what do we do now? Half the town knows where these folks are now. Pretty soon we'll be bringing in sightseers from out of state to look at 'em."

"Why the extreme secrecy, Uncle Miltie?" Gracie asked. "You didn't trust me? We could keep them in the house. There's room. And feed them decently."

"I knew the house was being watched, at least off and on. Or didn't you notice? I'm surprised they weren't out tonight."

"They don't work in the rain," Rocky joked.

Gracie had known that she was being followed, at least in the abstract, but it was easy to keep forgetting. It was such a silly thing, to follow a small-town widow around on her daily errands.

"Besides," Uncle Miltie continued, "they could come to the house with a search warrant anytime, if they thought Hannah and the boys might be there. Couldn't risk it. Especially with you being so chummy with the editor here, and the police chief, and that ATF woman and the others."

"So," Rocky concluded, "you can't take them in, Gracie, and I can tell by looking at you that you want to. The safest place for them, when all's said and done, is right here where they are."

Marge protested, "But it's so — so — primitive!"

Hannah said, "It's all right. We're getting enough to eat, and we have good fresh water out of a spigot outside, and Tim takes the toilet bucket out and empties it every night after dark. This can't last forever."

Gracie felt crushed. She apparently was less stouthearted about the insufficiencies than Hannah was. "So when I saw you behind the church, you were waiting for Uncle Miltie to come with the day's provisions."

Hannah nodded.

Rocky rubbed his eyes and stretched. It was a small, close place for so many people. "Well, we can't just sit around waiting for something nice to happen. We're going to have to make it happen."

"How?"

"I don't know. But we must. So we will."

36

Now here was a curious thing. Gracie didn't mind driving at all when Marge or some other woman sat beside her. But men on the car seat beside her made her nervous. Perhaps it came from clear back in those days when her father was teaching her to drive and would constantly bark corrections. Perhaps it meant she'd swallowed the myth that every American male deluded himself with, namely that he was a better-than-average driver.

Rocky sat beside her now, and it made her nervous. "Turn there and loop around at the next corner," he told her.

"Why do that?" Gracie asked.

"Because it's dumb and nobody would do it. Therefore, if anyone's following us, we'll know it."

She couldn't fault that logic. After she made the suggested maneuvers, they paused in an alleyway a moment to watch, then proceeded to the vacant house. Along the rail fence among the trees, Hannah and her two boys waited for them. Gracie pulled to the side of the little back street. The three climbed into Fannie Mae and immediately hunkered down in the backseat, invisible from outside.

"Where are we going?" Hannah's voice from the backseat was muffled.

Rocky replied, "Chicago."

Tim blew a raspberry. "Okay, now where are we *really* going?"

"Chicago," Gracie affirmed. "Keep your head down."

"All the way to Chicago?"

"No, just until we're out on the freeway and we're certain that no one's following."

"I don't understand," Hannah said. "Last night before you left, you said to be waiting early today, but I thought we'd be going somewhere around here. I don't think I want to go to Chicago."

"Yes, you do." Rocky pointed to a road sign. "Turn north here and you can cut off five miles of stoplights."

Ever ready to avoid stoplights, Gracie turned north on the state route.

"Hannah," Rocky explained, "I have a friend who's a tropical medicine specialist. We went to school together. He's practicing in Chicago now. I called him last night about Brad. He says the local doctors might be misdiagnosing because they're not looking for tropical parasitic diseases. What they'd treat your boy for isn't what he might have. So we're taking him in, let Sam get a look at him."

"I don't have any money."

"Sam does." And that ended that.

"What if someone sees me in Chicago?"

"I dropped by Herb Bower's, and he'd checked the court records. There's no warrant out on you. They want you for questioning, is all. So in Chicago, you should be able to move pretty freely. All the same, you'll be using a different name."

"I hope this isn't another one of those ideas that looks good and when you get into it, it turns out to be terrible." That was Gracie's contribution.

"Let's hope not," Rocky agreed. Gracie crossed her fingers in her lap.

They let Hannah and the boys sit up when they crossed the second county line. When they passed the place where Rick and Gracie had rescued Roberta Desmond, Gracie related that story in detail.

Turning on the radio, Rocky found that each traveler wanted a different kind of station. All the way to the city, Gracie's passengers never did find a station everyone agreed on.

Gracie's mind mulled over many things, but she only asked one question on the drive. "Why is Uncle Miltie letting Gooseberry come along with him to visit you?"

Hannah explained, "Brad had a cat in Bolivia and we had to leave it behind because it wasn't home when we left. It was half wild anyway. And then he got a kitten here but it disappeared. When George — the man you call Uncle Miltie — heard that, he said Brad could borrow his until he could get one of his own."

And that explained, probably, why Gooseberry had been behaving so weirdly recently. He often did that, Gracie now realized, when his ordinary routine was disrupted. She simply had failed to interpret his actions in the correct way.

As they entered Chicago, Rocky remarked, "I love this town. I should come more often."

"You should talk to Rick Harding. But now tell me where to go."

"I wouldn't dare." Rocky teased, but then he directed her. He was very good at it, too, warning her about exits and turns well in advance of her need for them.

Eventually, Gracie pulled into a parking tower taller than any building in Willow Bend. She found a spot on the third level and they walked across a glass bridge into one of the world's most extensive medical centers.

Rocky didn't need the building directory. He led his entourage directly to the elevators, got off on the eleventh floor, and conducted them down an endless, carpeted hall to a suite in a corner. He ushered them inside and bade them sit while he spoke to the receptionist.

The boys zeroed in instantly on a tropical fish tank. Hannah looked around at the opulence surrounding them. "If he heals with interior décor, Brad's well already."

Gracie laughed out loud. It was the first stab at humor she had ever heard from this unfortunate young woman, so it especially pleased her. "Nothing like it in Willow Bend."

"Or Bolivia. At least, that I ever saw."

Three other people sat quietly in this sumptuous waiting room, each of them apparently from countries other than the United States.

Rocky had no sooner sat down when his friend came bouncing out into the room from a side door. Dr. Sam Gillette embraced Rocky warmly.

Rocky introduced the tall, gray-templed

physician to everyone, telling Hannah, "We'll be back in a couple hours," and headed Gracie to the door.

Gracie glanced back as she left. Hannah stood there open-mouthed, as the boys asked questions about the fish. After the door had closed, she asked, "Isn't this a bit abrupt?"

"I told Sam the whole story last night. He said to give him three hours to examine the kid, run some tests, and all. So while we're waiting, I thought we'd go visit another friend of mine."

"This is all moving too fast for me." She headed for the elevators.

"I'm getting us a taxi now — we'll leave the car in the garage here."

"Your call," said Gracie.

Soon they were entering one of the glass office buildings downtown, and Gracie found herself ushered into a lair that Messrs. Grzbovsky and Patterson knew well — the regional FBI office.

"I didn't know you had friends in high FBI places," she told him.

"It's only in Willow Bend that I'm not appreciated." Rocky was escorting her through a spaghetti-tangle of rooms and cubicles to one particular office, where he rapped on the door and conducted her inside.

The man in that office rather resembled Rocky. Like Gracie's companion, he was sturdily built and gruff in outward demeanor. His white short-sleeved dress shirt, though, was crisp, a condition Rocky's shirts never managed to attain.

"Gracie Parks, this is Grover Wills. Grover, we've come to take you to lunch."

"I thought you'd never ask! Let me get my coat."

As Agent Wills turned away to retrieve his sport coat from a rack in the corner, Gracie couldn't help but notice the .38 holstered at the small of his back. It reminded her that, jocular though these two might be, they were dangerous. Both of them.

Rocky muttered loudly, "Now remember, Gracie. Just don't say anything about Muppets. He was named after one."

"Very funny." Grover Wills shrugged into his jacket. "Where we going? Same old place?"

"Unless you want to fight the noon traffic."

So they went downstairs to the office building's basement, which housed a food court. A dozen fast-food chain restaurants ringed the periphery of a large, open eating area with dainty white tables and chairs.

Gracie was not particularly sanguine about burgers unless she made them herself, but these two seemed to favor them, so she stood in line for a burger also. "I'm surprised there are so many people here."

"You should see it when it's busy." Grover moved forward a notch.

"Rocky?" Gracie asked. "What about Hannah and the boys?"

"No problem. Sam's going to feed them."

Grover turned to stare at Rocky. "You're not going to tell me the Hannah in question is Hannah Cates, right? Tell me it isn't so."

"It's so. Why do you think we're taking you to lunch? We want to know what's going on here."

Grover now wasn't smiling. "I was hoping you could tell me."

37

Gracie's El had claimed that "Nobody understands the police mind. That includes the police." He might have had to make an exception for Rocky. As she and these two old friends chatted at lunch, she watched Rocky and Grover blend into a seamless duo who finished each other's sentences and anticipated each other's lines.

Then Grover asked, "So what's with this Hannah Cates?"

"Gracie, you know her better than I do." Rocky paused. "It's safe."

And so Gracie related everything she knew about Hannah and her past, up to and including that discovery in the old garage. Rocky added a point or two here and there.

Grover took it in and pondered. "Interesting. So you think the family took to begging when they got back to the States from Bolivia?"

Rocky nodded. "Likely. Gracie and Hannah's story meshes well with what I dug up on them. It's also possible that while Hannah lives half a block from the church and Jason breaks into it to use the phone, neither knows the other is right there."

"Wouldn't that be something!" But Gracie allowed as how it could be. Hannah and the boys all had insisted they knew nothing of Jason's whereabouts.

"Or he's afraid he'd endanger them by leading the authorities to them inadvertently."

"*Or,*" Gracie was really getting into this, "or, someone else is pursuing him and them. They're hiding from someone in addition to federal agents."

"I'm worried." Rocky nudged her. "You're starting to think like a crook."

"Don't bug her. I like the way she thinks." Grover leaned closer. "The ostensible reason that Grzbovsky and Patterson are down there is to try to find some bozos who lifted an armored car and took it and its driver across state lines." He glanced at Gracie. "We can only become involved if it's interstate."

She nodded.

He continued. "At about the same time, we got this directive. Apparently a tall pile of funds was going to be earmarked for enforcement, but suddenly dried up. So the agencies who were supposed to be getting the money found themselves competing for a short pile."

"I think I heard something about that on TV," Gracie said.

"So all of a sudden, we find ourselves forced to spice up our reports, to make sure it's clear that we're the folks who can best use the money." He waved a hand. "Now I don't mean lie, or anything. We're supposed to just sound like the sharpest knife in the drawer. Know what I mean?"

Rocky picked it up. "And your guys in Willow Bend wound up getting carried away, trying to make a big international deal out of a simple heist. Right?"

"That's what it sounds like's happening."

"I wondered, when the crime was supposed to be arms, but Bolivia is not noted for gun-running. Bolivia is drugs, if anything." Gracie was catching on.

Grover said, "But drugs are no longer the darling of the legislature. Drugs are ho-hum. The hot-button issue now is going to be gun control. Everything's going to be arms for a while. So I'm sorry if my people down there got a little overzealous."

"A *little?!*" Rocky snorted.

Gracie laid a hand on Grover's arm. "If it makes you feel any better, those nice ATF people got carried away just as badly. They even put my uncle in a line-up."

"Now, Gracie," Rocky soothed. "She apologized. That still leaves almost a hundred thousand dollars unaccounted for. Think it's that heist?"

"Don't know." Grover shrugged. "Now if it was a hundred mil, that'd be some serious money. But a hundred Gs sounds more like a local job. Any banks around town missing funds lately?"

"No, just a pop machine."

"There you are." Grover straightened. "I need to go back to work one of these days."

"And we ought to pick up Hannah and the kids soon." Rocky stood up and started gathering their wrappers and cups.

Gracie stood up, too. "Do you suppose we can get back to Willow Bend by seven or so? There's a church board meeting tonight."

"Don't see why not."

"Tell you what," Grover said. "I'll get Grzbovsky on the phone for a little heart-to-heart talk. I don't have any control over ATF, but I can at least call a couple of people. For now your Cates family aren't fugitives from the FBI, and maybe we can save them from a few other agencies, too."

Gracie thanked him perhaps a little too profusely. But then, he didn't have any inkling whatever of what it must be like to hide with two children in an unheated garage.

They arrived at Willow Bend's city limits, the Cateses and all, at 7:55. Gracie said, "I'll take you home, Rocky, and drop these people off. I can still make the meeting in time."

"Drop them off, but I want to go into the meeting with you. It's not closed, is it?"

"No, it's open, but why? You're not —" she bit her lip. Since the Cateses were here, she changed it to "you're not a member."

"I know you. This could get real interesting. You have something in mind."

"Very well, then. Actually, I was going to drop you off and take the Cateses in with me. Will you do that, please, Hannah?"

Hannah stammered a bit, but she said yes. The boys were tired from the long outing — Brad, especially from the medical tests — but Hannah was too grateful to Gracie to argue. She knew, too, that it was possible their situation was about to change — and that it could only be for the better.

They pulled up to the church door at two minutes after eight. Gracie conducted Hannah and the boys directly to the conference room.

Pastor Paul was saying, "The first order of business is —" and stopped to stare at the entering group.

Gracie saw Uncle Miltie sitting at the far side of the room. She grinned. He grinned. She knew why he was here, and she was pretty sure he understood what she was about to do.

Gracie nodded at her pastor and began to speak.

"Fellow board members," she said, "I see my uncle is here. Good. He'll tell you, I'm sure, that he is furious that the church opted to put its building ahead of the needs of a desperate young woman. Because of that decision, he has been doing his best to help her, all by himself. He has been bringing food and other essentials to this woman and her hungry children, doing what he can and letting God fill in the rest. He can't drive, he can't get to the grocery store, his funds are severely limited. But he is doing what he can do."

Uncle Miltie stood up. "Jesus always put people first. Always. The church is supposed to be reflecting Jesus. And you'll be the first to agree, Paul, that God honors the heart. If the church does what it's supposed to be doing, God will take care of it. That's what's called 'faith'!"

Gracie stepped aside. "Ladies and gentlemen, Hannah Cates here is going to tell you her story. Oh, wait. First, some good news. A specialist in tropical medicine, now practicing in Chicago, has diagnosed her son with a curable infection and started him on a medication that should make him well. His mother has been fearing for his life."

"How much did it cost?" Uncle Miltie asked.

"Free. I suggest, my friends, that was more than a gift from God to Hannah. It is a sign from God that He can do whatever is necessary. Now, hear Hannah. Ask her questions as you wish. And then, dear fellow board members, we will talk about making a major adjustment in our priorities."

38

As church board meetings went, this one was a doozy. Instead of falling asleep, which Gracie too often felt like doing, she found her attention glued to the guest speaker.

Hannah was eloquent in her sweet, southern way. The story she told here departed very little from the one Gracie had heard earlier. Rocky was nodding as he jotted notes. When she finished, the room sat hushed, but for the feverish scratching of Estelle's pencil.

Jessica Larson asked, "Comments?"

"Yes." Uncle Miltie stood up and pulled some crudely folded papers from his pocket. "Same story she told me, but with fewer details. Now here are the notes that Pastor Paul mislaid a couple weeks ago when he was describing the church's financial situation."

"Aha!" Paul watched him lay them on the table.

Undaunted, Uncle Miltie continued. "They're a very good summary of what we need and where the needs are. But they leave out the most important service. To people. As a lay church member I propose, as I have the constitutional right to do, that the church maintain its present budget for aid and welfare and ask God for the rest, having every confidence that He'll provide."

Jessica sighed heavily.

Fred Baxter growled, "That's not a sound way to do business." He was, after all, a banker.

"Depends on what the business is," said Gracie. "Banks are limited to secular resources. We're not."

Hannah added, "I didn't have much faith when we ended up here. But I see now how real everyday faith operates. I have what I need — even Bradley does. I don't —"

Jessica opened her mouth to speak.

"Daddy!" Little Brad leaped up and ran out the open door. His face alight, Tim raced after him.

Rocky glanced at Gracie and bolted for the door. Gracie followed quickly behind him.

Jason Cates stood on his knees, his arms wrapped around his sons, and he was weeping.

Someone jostled Gracie. She gasped. "Grover Mills!"

"Decided to come down and check us out in person, eh?" Rocky asked.

"Yeah. See if I could salvage this mess." Grover stepped forward and presented his badge to Jason. "You, Cates. Want to tell us about it?"

Jason climbed to his feet and took a profoundly deep breath. His wife was wrapped tightly against him now. He wiped his eyes. "Don't know if you'll believe me."

"Go for it."

"We were desperate for money. Really desperate. Begging with a cardboard sign doesn't do it when you have two hungry kids and one of them sick. These two guys asked me to go in with them in, ah, relieving a truck of a little cash it didn't need. Their plan sounded pretty foolproof. So I asked Hannah to hang around Willow Bend until I came for her. I didn't tell her what I was doing."

"Name the two."

"They're not from around here. Anyway, we pulled it off. I was surprised how easy it was. But at the same time I felt guilty. And I thought what would happen to Hannah and the kids if I got caught, and how they'd been loyal to me all along and now —" He almost started crying again.

Gracie's eyes felt hot.

He continued, "So I stole the money from those two and ran. I hitched a ride into Willow Bend here, but I needed somewhere to hide, and fast. I tried the church window and bingo, I was in. So I hid the cash in that attic closet because there was a layer of dust on its door handle."

"Pretty smart." Rocky was taking notes rapidly.

"Now I had to hide from the cops *and* from those two. I didn't know where Hannah was, but I didn't want her with me anyway, until it all settled out. I was trying to find out how to return the money to the company we lifted it off of, but then that twister came through." He shrugged helplessly. "All downhill from there."

Grover snorted. "I don't see any uphills in this whole sordid mess."

I do! Thank You, Lord! Gracie's heart was singing. *Thank You, Lord! Hannah and the boys are clear, and Jason's honest, at the root. Please see him through this now. Please!*

"You're under arrest, Cates. Anything you s—"

Hannah was being brave, but tears ran down her cheeks.

"Just a moment." Pastor Paul stepped

forward. "I understand you must arrest him. He broke the law. But he was trying to patch the break. And if his story checks out, we as a church would like to sponsor him. There's a program for that in this state, you know."

"This is a federal arrest."

"We'll fight about jurisdiction later. The bottom line is, Hannah says he's a great handyman. That's how he got the job in Bolivia. He can fix anything. And what this church needs right now is a first-class handyman who can make extensive repairs." He studied Grover expectantly.

"Crazy." Grover stared at the pastor. "He's the perp but I'm the one in the hot seat. Okay. No promises, but I'll see what I can do." He turned to Rocky. "And my people are under orders to pack up and go find some other town to pester."

Jessica Larson called out, "The board is still in session! To call this irregular is understating it."

But nobody was listening.

"Barb isn't going to be here again tonight." Gracie addressed the rehearsing choir, baton in hand. "She asked me to take over. We can practice down here in the sanctuary, since Amy again asked, and that seems to be what everyone prefers."

She arranged the music in her stand. She didn't mind conducting, but she really preferred singing. She especially liked this piece.

The choir murmured among themselves. She waited for them to quiet down, but the noise grew.

She raised her voice. "Shall we?"

The murmuring ceased. Why did everyone look so expectant?

"Gracie," Don reminded her, "you remember what happened the last time you tried to lead."

"Very funny." She smiled and let it go. "The anthem this week is 'Ye Watchers and Ye Holy Ones.' Let's run through it from the top."

She raised her baton.

As one, the whole choir ducked under the pews.

Recipe

Grilled Chicken with Hoisin Marinade

- ✓ 1 teaspoon fresh or 1/2 teaspoon dried thyme leaves
- ✓ 6 tablespoons hoisin sauce
- ✓ 4 tablespoons rice vinegar
- ✓ 2 tablespoons olive oil
- ✓ Four chicken breast halves, boned

Mix first four ingredients to make marinade, and rub into each chicken breast on both sides. Put in a container with any extra marinade and cover with plastic wrap. Marinate for thirty minutes at room temperature or one hour in the refrigerator. If refrigerated, bring to room temperature before grilling.

When the grill is hot, quickly grill the chicken on both sides, basting with extra marinade. Be careful not to overcook. Serves two to four people.

As Gracie suspected, hoisin sauce is a good addition to chicken. Thinning the sauce with rice vinegar and olive oil makes sure that the flavor of the chicken will not be overwhelmed. After grilling, you can serve the breasts hot or cold, or cut into strips in a salad.

About the Author

When it comes to twisters, Sandy Dengler knows whereof she speaks. She now resides in Norman, Oklahoma, tornado alley. Born in Ohio, she married a National Park Service ranger and spent the rest of her life traveling and living in beautiful places such as Death Valley, Yosemite, Mount Rainier and Acadia. She and her husband Bill raised two daughters, Alyce and Mary, who now live in the Puget Sound area of Washington state with their families.

By day Sandy is a mild-mannered free-lance writer. By night, she builds dinosaurs and other paleo beasts for Oklahoma's new natural history museum. In between, she enjoys her hobbies of working on a variety of needlework and painting projects. She earned a bachelor's degree in zoology at Bowling Green State University and a master's degree in desert ecology at Arizona State University in Tempe.

As a child, Sandy dreamt of becoming a paleontologist. But little farm girls in rural Ohio in the 1940s and 1950s didn't even think about earning a doctorate in a man's profession. Fifty years later, with her husband's encouragement, she is pursuing that dream. She has commenced study at the University of Oklahoma with an eye toward a Ph.D. in paleontology.

The employees of Thorndike Press hope you have enjoyed this Large Print book. All our Thorndike and Wheeler Large Print titles are designed for easy reading, and all our books are made to last. Other Thorndike Press Large Print books are available at your library, through selected bookstores, or directly from us.

For information about titles, please call:
   (800) 223-1244
or visit our Web site at:
   www.gale.com/thorndike
   www.gale.com/wheeler

To share your comments, please write:

   Publisher
   Thorndike Press
   295 Kennedy Memorial Drive
   Waterville, ME   04901

Guideposts magazine and the *Daily Guide-posts* annual devotional book are available in large-print editions by contacting:
   Guideposts Customer Service
   39 Seminary Hill Road
   Carmel, NY 10512
or
   www. guideposts.org
or
   1-800-431-2344